The

Memory Keeper

THE SECOND FREAK HOUSE TRILOGY
#1

C.J. ARCHER

Other books by C.J. Archer:

The Wrong Girl (The 1st Freak House Trilogy #1)

Playing With Fire (The 1st Freak House Trilogy #2)

Heart Burn (The 1st Freak House Trilogy #3)

The Medium (Emily Chambers Spirit Medium #1)

Possession (Emily Chambers Spirit Medium #2)

Evermore (Emily Chambers Spirit Medium #3)

Her Secret Desire (Lord Hawkesbury's Players #1)

Scandal's Mistress (Lord Hawkesbury's Players #2)

To Tempt The Devil (Lord Hawkesbury's Players #3)

Honor Bound (The Witchblade Chronicles #1)

Kiss Of Ash (The Witchblade Chronicles #2)

The Charmer (Assassins Guild #1)

The Rebel (Assassins Guild #2)

The Saint (Assassins Guild #3)

Redemption

Surrender

FOR

You, my readers. Enjoy!

CHAPTER 1

Hertfordshire, Spring 1889

"What do you want to be goin' to Freak House for, miss?" asked the driver as he hauled my valise onto the rear of his wagon.

"*Freak* House?" I scrutinized his moustache for any signs of mirth, since I couldn't see the mouth beneath it. The unkempt shrubbery didn't so much as twitch. "Perhaps I didn't make myself clear. My destination is Frakingham House. Please tell me this is the village of Harborough." I looked back to the railway station. The handful of passengers who'd alighted the train alongside me had dispersed and the locomotive was long gone. Not even a wisp of steam remained in the cool air of dusk. Only the stationmaster remained on the platform, fob watch in hand. The sign beside him confirmed that I hadn't made a mistake.

The wagon driver chuckled. "Aye, this is Harborough and it's Frakingham House I'll be takin' you to, if that's where you wish to go." He held out his hand to me. "We local folk sometimes call it that. No harm meant, no harm done, eh?"

I accepted his assistance and stepped up, settling myself on the driver's seat; there was nowhere else to sit. I'd been lucky to secure the small wagon at all. I'd expected Jack or Samuel to meet me, but I hadn't recognized anyone on the platform. After inquiring of the stationmaster if one of the waiting coaches or carts belonged to Frakingham House, and having been informed that they did not, he'd hailed a passing driver on his way out of the village. The stationmaster assured me the fellow was reliable and honest, but if I preferred to wait for word to be sent to Frakingham House to send Mr. Langley's carriage to fetch me, then I was welcome to sit in the waiting room. I reluctantly took the offer of the passerby. It would be dark soon and driving in the dark could be even more perilous than sitting beside and aged and crooked little man.

The driver gathered up the reins and urged his horse forward. "I'm Billings. What's yer name, miss?"

"Charity. Charity Evans."

"And what's a pretty girl like you wantin' with them… uh, people up at Freak House, eh?"

Were all country folk nosey? Nobody in London would be so impertinent. "I have an acquaintance there."

"Mrs. Langley or Miss Langley? Both seem nice enough, although Miss Langley don't give me the time o' day. Mrs. Langley was ill some months back, before she married, but I saw her looking bonny again just the other day."

I allowed him to talk on and did not correct him. It was neither Mrs. Hannah Langley nor Miss Sylvia Langley whom I'd come to meet. I knew them both, however, and they were friendly enough, although Sylvia was somewhat aloof towards me. I supposed that was to be expected considering she had both feet firmly on one of the upper rungs of society and I didn't even have a toe-hold on the bottom one. It didn't matter. I only hoped she wouldn't make Hannah feel uncomfortable for inviting me. I didn't want to cause trouble between the two of them now that they were related through marriage.

I inhaled deeply, breathing in the fresh country air, and resisted the urge to remove my hat and let the breeze loosen my hair. Instead, I clamped a hand down on the crown to keep it from flying off. "If you don't mind," I told Billings, "I'd like to observe the countryside in peace until we reach the house. The evening is quite lovely for driving."

"That it is, miss, that it is." He mercifully didn't ask any more questions.

Indeed, it was I who asked him one several minutes later as we turned off the main road and drove through enormous iron gates. "Have we arrived?"

"Aye, miss. The house is looking like its old self again now that it's been fixed. The fire did some damage, but you can't tell no more."

As he finished speaking, the house came into view at the end of the long drive. My breath caught in my throat at the magnificent sight. I knew the owner, Mr. August Langley, was a wealthy man, but seeing his house hammered home just how wealthy. The majestic building stamped its importance on the surrounding landscape of green lawns and hedges like a glowering king. Its chimneys stretched toward the sky, as if they would rip out the clouds and replace them with gray smoke. A medieval knight wouldn't look out of place striding behind the crenellated turrets, nor would a forlorn maiden sitting in the window embrasure of one of the towers.

A shiver slithered down my spine. I may like Jack and Hannah Langley, but their house sent doubts burrowing into my mind. It seemed to be the sort of place where shadows lingered, even on a bright day, and whispers echoed when no one was about. It seemed a fitting residence for a man like Jack's uncle, August Langley. I'd been told the scientist conducted his experiments in a laboratory inside; what those experiments were, I didn't know, nor did I wish to find out.

"I heard about the fire," I muttered. The sound of my own voice roused me and I looked away from the house. We drove down an avenue of trees. Beyond the row to our right, the crumbling walls of a ruin crept to the edge of a lake. The water sparkled beneath the last rays of sunshine. A dense wood stretched behind it, almost up to the side of the house. If one did not look at the house itself, it was otherwise a tranquil country scene.

But the house could not be ignored. It demanded attention, and I was glad I wouldn't be staying long. As soon as Samuel Gladstone erased some of my memories, I would leave.

Billings drew the horses to a halt and stepped down from the seat. He saw to my valise as I looked up at the arched front door, with its thick iron hinges and knocker. I shivered again. The door alone made me feel quite small.

"Want me to stay until someone comes?" Billings asked, glancing at the western horizon where the sun had begun its descent.

"Thank you, but no. I'm expected."

He gave the door a dubious look. "Don't seem like it."

"I assure you, I am."

He shrugged and trudged back to his wagon. "I best be goin' anyway. The wife'll have supper waitin'."

I thanked him and lifted my hand to knock. The door was opened before I could put fist to wood. A tall, handsome man with dark hair stood just inside. He blinked back at me, a rather stupid expression on his face. Then he grinned.

"Charity!"

We did an awkward little dance where he bowed while I went to hug him. We laughed. "It's so good to see you, Tommy. Look at you in your work suit. You look like a penguin."

"Seen many penguins in London?" He laughed again. "I thought you weren't coming until tomorrow." He glanced past me to where the wagon rattled away up the drive. "Who was that?"

"A man from the village named Billings kindly offered to drive me from the station. What made you think I was coming tomorrow? My letter clearly stated the eighteenth. Today is the eighteenth."

"Clearly?" he mimicked. "Are you sure?"

I did not press the issue. Perhaps I'd not written the date well enough to be understood. My penmanship was something I needed to work on if I wanted to fit in at Frakingham House. That and not falling back into the London cant of my youth.

I tugged on my cuffs, more out of habit than any real attempt to hide the scars on the backs of my hands. The sleeves were long and I wore gloves anyway. The tugging was something I did when I was anxious. Hopefully my nerves would settle once the memories of the events that had caused the scars were erased.

"Come inside," Tommy said. "The others will be pleased to see you."

He picked up my valise and deposited it at the base of a set of stairs that swept up to a landing then split off in opposite directions. My gaze followed the ascent of the supporting stone arches and columns to the vaulted octagonal ceiling high above. If I felt small near the front door, I felt distinctly miniature in the entrance hall.

"It can be overwhelming at first," Tommy said quietly. "You get used to it."

"It reminds me of a cathedral."

"Mr. Langley wouldn't want to hear that. He doesn't even like going to church on Sundays." He winked. "Come on, I'll take you to Jack and the others."

I untied my hat and removed my gloves. "Is that how you address all your guests?" I asked, setting hat and gloves on my valise.

"Only the ones I knew from before."

Before. Before he became footman at Frakingham House. Before Jack became August Langley's nephew. Before. I remembered that time. It wasn't all bad. Thanks to Jack's unusual ability to set fire to anything, and his nimble fingers, we'd been warm, had food in our bellies, and nobody had bothered us. I liked "before." It was the time *after*, when Tommy and Jack had gone, that I was keen to forget.

I went to tug on my sleeves again, but caught myself and stopped. "Lead the way, Dawson," I said, calling him by his surname as masters called their servants.

"I'm just Tommy here." He smiled and I smiled back. It felt odd that he was a servant in the house where I was a guest, yet I was happy that he had good employment.

That was important for people like us. People who'd come from nowhere and who had nothing. I too had good work at the school. I felt valued there. It was why I wanted to give it my best, my all. To do that, I needed to be free of the nightmares that kept me awake. I couldn't wait to return to the children in my care. I hoped they didn't miss me too much. Well, perhaps a little. Enough to know that I was wanted.

He led me through an arched door, along a short corridor to another. He entered first and stepped to the side, giving me a view of Jack, Hannah, Sylvia and Samuel sitting at a card table. I expected Tommy to announce my name formally, but there was no time for him to say anything.

"Charity!" Hannah cried. "You're here!" She leapt up and rushed to embrace me.

"You're early," Jack said, kissing my cheek after his wife let me go. "I thought you weren't coming until tomorrow."

"Today," I told him. "The eighteenth." Next time I would write the date in words rather than numbers to avoid misunderstandings.

Sylvia did not get up, but smiled politely and welcomed me. It was clear from the lack of warmth in her greeting that she didn't like having a woman of dubious moral character in her drawing room. Perhaps she thought I would sully the furniture with my breath or some such nonsense. There were women out there with those views. I should know, I'd encountered many.

Samuel approached and extended his hand to take mine. I held back, but not out of habit this time. Being near

Samuel, with all his handsome perfection, reminded me how ugly my scars were. Yet it was more than that. For some reason, Samuel made me aware of how low I was, how uneducated and uncouth. It wasn't his fault; he'd always behaved in a gentlemanly way toward me. The combination of his charm and hypnotism made me nervous, however. I planned on spending as little time in his company as possible.

A flicker of surprise marred his smooth brow then he bowed. When he straightened, he was once more the smiling gentleman. There was no hint that he thought me odd for keeping my hands to myself. He would learn the reason for the scars soon enough.

"Hello, Charity," he finally said. He was an extraordinarily handsome man with sky-blue eyes, tousled sandy hair and a ready smile. Indeed, he was almost too handsome, at least for me. It was those types of gentlemen who'd gotten me into trouble before.

"I'm sorry I wasn't there to meet you," he went on. "The stationmaster should have sent word."

"There wasn't time," I said. "It grew late. Besides, a very pleasant man named Billings drove me."

"Pleasant? You mean he didn't chew off your ear with gossip?"

Sylvia pulled a face. "If he's been saying things about us again, I'll… I'll see that he regrets it."

"I told him I was too tired for conversation," I said quickly.

"Syl, don't worry about what others are saying," Jack chided his cousin. "Billings is harmless. Besides, he has no idea what we do up here. If he did, he'd probably be saying far worse things than merely calling us freaks."

I swallowed. What *was* Mr. Langley concocting in his laboratory? It was bad enough knowing Jack could start fires at any moment and Samuel could get a woman—indeed, anyone—to do his will with a few spoken words, but at least I knew what they were capable of and I trusted them to control themselves. I knew so little about August Langley. Despite having asked Jack in the past, he'd not told me what his uncle was working on. If it was a cure for disease, why wouldn't he say?

"Jack, stop it," Sylvia snapped. "It's not a joke. You may not mind being called a freak, since you are one, but I'm not and nor is Hannah, anymore."

"Thank you," Hannah said, wryly. "She's right though, Jack. You're scaring Charity." She hooked her arm through mine. "I can assure you, we're all quite normal. Even Bollard."

"Bollard?"

"August's assistant. You'll meet him at dinner."

"I'm sure you'd like to go to your room to freshen up," Sylvia said to me.

"I'll take you," Hannah offered. "Tommy will bring your valise."

"I will," Samuel said.

Sylvia clicked her tongue. "Don't be ridiculous. It's Tommy's job, not yours. Good lord," she muttered. "A pretty woman comes to stay and suddenly none of the men remember their proper place."

I'm sure her words were meant to scold Samuel, but her gaze wandered over Tommy before returning to me. I looked down at my feet to hide my reddening face. I hoped I hadn't made an enemy of her already. Then again, I suspected the things she didn't like about me were the things I couldn't change—my background and my appearance. I'd been called everything from pretty to striking, and not always in a kindly tone. I did try to keep my blonde hair tightly bound, and I usually only wore black or gray to avoid drawing attention to myself. Some women liked to be seen and hated being ignored; I wanted to blend in and be left alone.

"Don't mind Sylvia," Hannah said to me as we walked back towards the entrance hall. "She can be a little petty, sometimes. It's best to ignore her. Don't you agree, Tommy?"

"I find Miss Langley impossible to ignore," he said from behind us. "She's very, uh, noticeable."

Hannah giggled and squeezed my arm as if sharing a secret with me, but I had no idea what it could be. I'm sure Tommy was speaking with the utmost respect for his mistress and was referring to her pretty face and golden hair, not her bold personality.

"I am so glad you agreed to come," Hannah said as we walked side-by-side up the grand staircase. Our footfalls were somewhat deadened by the plush crimson carpet covering the steps, but our voices echoed. "I wasn't sure if you would, at first, and I admit that your letter consenting to the scheme came as a surprise. A pleasant one, I might add. I do think it'll work."

My skin prickled at the thought of the path I was about to take. Although I was determined to go through with the hypnosis to remove some of my memories, the thought of being entirely under another person's spell, even for just a few moments, sent cold fingers of fear wrapping around my insides. Particularly when the one casting the spell, so to speak, was a man, and a charming, handsome one at that. I'd sworn to avoid men like Samuel Gladstone.

At least I would be among friends with Jack, Hannah and Tommy. Especially Jack. Of everyone, he knew me best. He knew my weaknesses, my fears, my hopes and dreams. He even knew a little about my nightmares and what caused them, but not in great detail. It was after talking to him at a Christmas ball held by my employers, the Beauforts, that the idea of hypnosis was first mentioned. Nothing more came of it for some weeks, while Hannah battled her illness and they raced to find a cure. It was only two weeks ago, after their wedding, that they had been in London and we once again met up at the Beauforts' house, for a celebratory dinner. The wedding had been an intimate affair with only the residents of Frakingham House in attendance. Hannah had not even invited her guardian, Lord Wade. She and Jack wrote to the Beauforts, Culverts and me after the event, expressing their desire to call upon us all as the new Mr. and Mrs. Langley. It had been a lovely evening, even though I felt somewhat out of place being the only one not residing in a grand mansion. With such kind people surrounding me, I was quickly put at ease again. It was testament to the humble upbringings of not only Hannah and Jack, but also Mrs. Beaufort, too.

It was also a testament to Hannah's love and trust in her husband that she accepted me as a friend so readily. My history with Jack was such that she had every right to hate being in my presence. I wasn't sure I'd be so accepting of my husband's prior lover.

Jack was my first and I was his. We'd been far too young for all of that, but we hadn't known any better, with no adults of good moral fiber to guide us. Nor did we know what we were doing, at first; it just seemed like the natural thing to do under the circumstances. Besides, everyone was doing it in our circle of abandoned and orphaned children. Perhaps if we'd waited things would have worked out differently between us, but then again, he was deliriously happy with his new wife and I was no longer in love with him, so it would seem everything worked out well enough. Still, I wished I'd held onto my virtue longer. It may have led me to make different choices, and I'd made some terrible ones in the past.

But that was all behind me now. Or it would be, after Samuel hypnotized me.

Tommy deposited my valise on the floor near the bed and left us. The housekeeper arrived with a maid and quickly prepared the room. They lit a small fire in the grate then they too left.

"Do you need assistance to change for dinner?" Hannah asked.

"No, thank you. My dress is simple enough that I can manage on my own." I tried not to admire her dress as I said it, but it was quite impossible. It may have been a day gown, but it was not something I'd ever worn. It was a deep blue that set off the red of her hair beautifully. The fabric draped across the front of the skirt was embellished with a knotted fringe and braided trim in cream. It must have cost more than my monthly wage, which was quite generous for a mere teacher.

"The chill should disappear soon, now that the fire is lit," she said, stoking it. She paused and laughed. "It's ironic, isn't it? I used to hate the warmth, now I can never seem to be warm enough."

"You are quite well, now?" I asked, somewhat hesitantly. It wasn't polite conversation to discuss illness, particularly of the nature that Hannah's had been. She seemed quite open about it, and indeed spoke freely of the events that led to the cure when I'd last seen her at the Beauforts' townhouse. Until then, I hadn't been aware of her fire starting. They'd kept that information from me, to protect me. Jack knew her ability would frighten me, as his had of late.

"Yes, thank you," she said. "Fortunately there's been no relapse. Mr. Langley—August—has ordered me to remain here for a few more days, so that he can observe me, but as soon as he gives me a clean bill of health, Jack and I will be off on our honeymoon."

"I'm so happy for you," I said. "For you both. I've never seen Jack more content."

She took my hands in her own. I let her, something I rarely did. "Thank you, Charity. It means a lot to hear you say it. I know how much he means to you, and you to him. I promise to take good care of him."

I laughed. "He led me to believe he's the one taking care of you."

"He *would* say that. He's a man." She winked. "I'll have Samuel escort you down to dinner at eight. Will that give you long enough?"

"Ample, but... please just send a maid. There's no need to trouble Samuel. Or anyone else," I quickly added. "Indeed, I'm sure I'll find my way on my own." Dear lord, could I sound more like a dim-wit? I blamed Samuel. He was making me nervous and he wasn't even there.

She winked again and smiled. My entire body cringed in horror; she thought I *liked* Samuel. I wanted to tell her that it wasn't the case and that he made me anxious, but then I would have to tell her why. And I didn't know why. It wasn't something I could fathom, let alone explain.

"I hope my early arrival hasn't upset the household," I said. "The mix-up was entirely my fault. I was sure I wrote the eighteenth in my letter to Jack, but I must have written the nineteenth."

"Eighteenth, nineteenth, what's one day? We're glad you're here. All of us." She winked again.

Time to change the subject. "Hannah, may I ask you something?"

"Of course."

"Samuel hypnotized you once, didn't he?"

She nodded. "When he worked for a London hypnotist. It was how we met. It turned out that Dr. Werner was a fraud, but Samuel is quite legitimate."

"Did he... did it hurt?"

"Not at all. I didn't feel anything. It was like falling asleep then waking up again."

"But... were you *aware* of Samuel? Could you... feel him inside your head?"

"No, nothing. Charity, are you quite sure you want to do this?"

"Yes. My mind is even more made up, now that you've assured me you didn't even know he was there."

"We-ell." She bit her lip and winced. "I should confess that when Samuel hypnotized me, he could not get into my mind. Not like he can with other people. He told me he was met with a wall that he couldn't break through. You see, a memory block had already been put there and that stopped any further exploration under hypnosis. *Your* mind will be open to Samuel. If you're not prepared for him to see your memories, then you shouldn't go through with it."

I touched the scar on the back of my right hand. It was the worst of the two. The skin from my knuckles to my wrist puckered like a prune. It had been painful at the time, but not as painful as watching a man die. The man who'd been my lover, my benefactor, my tormentor. The man who would soon be obliterated from my memories.

CHAPTER 2

"I'm ready," I assured Hannah. "It doesn't matter what Samuel discovers, anyway. I'll never see him again, after I leave."

She frowned. "Why do you think that?"

"We're unlikely to cross paths again. There's simply no reason to."

"But..." She sighed. "Never mind." She gently clasped my arm. "If you have any doubts about the process, you should speak to Samuel beforehand. And Charity, you must be absolutely certain that you want to block the memories. There will be consequences. If you want to discuss it further, you must seek me out."

"Thank you, but I've thought it through and this is what I want."

"Well, then. I'm glad." She left and I was finally alone again. I'd hardly had five minutes to myself since closing the door to my bedroom at the school. It was less than half the size of the guest bedroom I now found myself in, and far less opulent. The curtains alone were of better quality than any of my dresses, and the fireplace was enormous, with a heavily carved black mantel surrounding it. I was grateful the maid had lit only a small fire in it; perhaps the servants had been warned about my aversion to them.

They must think me odd. Indeed, most people probably thought me strange. I was too tall and too thin, for one thing. For another, I wasn't a typical teacher. I didn't have any formal education, never having gone to school myself, and I couldn't remember much of my family. Jack, Tommy and the others had been my family growing up, and now the school and students meant everything to me. All of them were orphans, like myself, and all of them were in need of love and support. I was capable of giving them the latter, but it was the former that eluded me. It hadn't always, I'd loved my little family of fellow orphans growing up, and they'd loved me in return. I lost the ability to love after *that*. *He'd* destroyed that part of me.

Tomorrow I was going to reclaim it, with Samuel's help.

***

August Langley had the soft, insipid features of a man unfamiliar with the outdoors. Apparently he rarely left his rooms, even to greet visitors, and I could believe it; he hardly spoke to anyone at dinner, let alone me. He was polite enough, asking me about my journey and the school, but I didn't think he was listening to my answers. Perhaps that was how geniuses behaved, as nobody else at the table seemed particularly embarrassed by his lack of manners, although Sylvia did cough rather loudly when he went for a long stretch without even a nod of acknowledgement.

The hulking, silent assistant didn't help matters. Bollard served his wheelchair-bound master then remained behind him for the rest of the meal, as still and blank-faced as a Tower of London guard. My gaze kept wandering to him, hoping to catch him looking at me or smiling at the lively conversation between Jack, Hannah and Samuel, but he never flinched.

What made the meal even more uncomfortable was that Tommy served us. It felt awkward. He was my friend, and Jack's too; we had known each other a long time. He used to pull my hair and teach me rude jokes. We'd worked as a team to steal bread and apples to fill our bellies. We'd seen the worst of each other, and the best, and there'd been no secrets between us, back then. The only time he'd served me was when I'd twisted my ankle at age thirteen and he'd handed me a plate laden with whatever food could be scrounged that day. It was not only odd to have him serve me like this, but just as odd that it seemed to bother neither him nor Jack. Perhaps it was an arrangement they'd simply grown accustomed to. It had been years since they'd moved here, Jack as Langley's nephew and Tommy as the footman. Jack had offered to find me a place as a maid, but I'd refused. I wasn't interested in being anyone's servant then, and I still wasn't.

Sometimes I wonder how different my life would have been if I'd accepted his offer. I wouldn't be in a permanent state of anxiety, for one thing, but then I wouldn't have ended up a teacher at the orphan school either.

"I must return to my work," August Langley announced, almost as soon as he'd swallowed his final mouthful of pudding. "Before I go, I need to ask you if you fully understand what you're asking Samuel to do, Miss Evans?"

His statement took me by surprise. Not only did it have nothing to do with him, but he'd shown no interest in my welfare all evening. "I have thoroughly thought it through," I told him. "I know that losing some memories may change my perspective on life. You must understand, Mr. Langley, that is precisely the reason I wish to go through with this." I chose my words carefully. I wasn't sure whether Jack had told anyone the sort of memories I was going to have erased. I doubted it. He knew how important privacy was to me in this matter. Besides, he didn't know the full extent of it himself. No one did.

"Our memories are what make us, Miss Evans. The good and the bad. They remind us of the mistakes we've made and help guide which paths we choose in the future. If we only have good memories, we may be destined to repeat those mistakes."

"Or we may not, now that we're older and wiser." Although I knew he meant well, I bristled at his lecture. I was two and twenty years of age. I'd been taking care of myself since I was nine. I didn't need the advice of someone who hardly knew me and knew nothing of my situation. "Jack, you understand, don't you?"

"I think so," he said. He shifted in his chair and looked down at his empty bowl. "But there could be ramifications that we haven't yet thought of. I just hope it's worth it."

I blinked at him. How could he not think *me* worth it? Because that was what was at stake. Me. My life. My future. My ability to love and be loved. I wanted to feel again. Wanted to feel happiness and wholeness so very much that it burned within me. But, no matter how hard I tried, I could not. I knew the capacity was in me somewhere, but it was deeply buried under the horrible memories. Hot tears stung my eyes. I looked away so no one could see them.

"I understand," Hannah said, somewhat vehemently. "Don't blame the men for their lack of empathy."

"Don't lump me in with your ignorant husband," Samuel said, cheerfully. I had to applaud him for trying to steer the conversation away from the heated turn it had taken, but his chivalry may have come too late.

"Perhaps there are some things only a woman can comprehend," Hannah said to me. "The world is, after all, controlled by men. How can they fully understand what it's like to have no control, and no means of protection against the more unscrupulous of their sex?"

She *did* understand. I should have known she would. She'd been held prisoner, for most of her life, in an attic by her guardian—a man. In some ways, it was good to see that she'd come through her ordeal unscathed. It meant there was hope for me.

"I'm not sure I want to be in control of everything," Sylvia said, with a toss of her blonde curls. "I know I don't want to drive a coach, for example. Or manage investments and estates. Too many numbers give me a headache."

"Do you want to choose whom you marry?" Hannah challenged. "Or what you do with *your* money?"

"I don't have any money."

"If you had control over your own life, you could earn it."

She wrinkled her nose. "Good lord, Hannah, you do say the oddest things. Why would I *want* to work?"

Hannah sighed heavily and appealed to Tommy, oddly enough. He stood by the sideboard awaiting instructions and didn't flicker so much as an eyelash.

"I pity your future husband, Syl," Jack said with a chuckle.

"You're the one who should be pitied. Hannah's got some radical ideas."

He laughed and placed his hand over his wife's, diffusing the tension in the room. Sylvia still pouted, but I at least felt easier.

Langley beckoned his servant with a crook of his finger. The mute took the handles of the wheelchair and backed it away from the table.

"It's an interesting experiment," Langley said, as he was steered towards the door. "I'll be there as an observer. You don't mind if I make notes, Miss Evans?"

"I, uh, was hoping that I would be alone with Samuel and Jack," I said. Samuel had to be there, of course, since he was the only one who could perform the trick, but I wanted Jack there too. I trusted him more than I trusted anyone in the world. Certainly more than I trusted the too-charming Samuel Gladstone. I needed Jack there to ensure Samuel only performed the job he'd been tasked to do.

Langley put a hand up and Bollard stopped. I'd turned to watch them go and now had my back to the other diners. Langley frowned at me, then his gaze shifted behind me to where Jack and Hannah sat. He nodded. "As you wish. Go, Bollard."

Bollard wheeled him out. It seemed as if everyone in the room took a deep breath at the same time.

"I'm sorry about my uncle," Jack said. "He's not used to guests. He doesn't leave the house much and we get few visitors."

"Pitifully few," Sylvia muttered. "Come with me, Hannah, Charity. We'll retreat to the drawing room while Jack and Samuel smoke and drink."

"I think we'll dispense with the usual formalities," Jack said. "We hardly ever separate after dinner anymore and it's only Charity, after all."

I smiled. It was so like Jack to treat me as one of the family and not a guest. I much preferred it too.

Sylvia huffed. "Can we please maintain some standards? You and Hannah may prefer informality, but Samuel and I do not."

"Speak for yourself," Samuel said. "I'd much rather stay and talk to the ladies than Jack. Believe me, the conversation is more riveting."

"Really?" Hannah's tone was teasing. "You wish to discuss petticoats and fashion?"

Sylvia made a choking sound and blushed. "Hannah, really. Not in front of the men."

Samuel laughed. "We are sorry, Charity," he said. "We've settled into our ways here and habits are hard to break. Jack's right. We're not used to company."

"Particularly not your sort," Sylvia said.

Hannah glared at her. Jack quickly apologized for her and Samuel echoed it. Sylvia blinked owlishly, and then finally seemed to comprehend that her flippant comment had sounded a little cruel.

"I meant teachers," she protested. "We're not used to *teachers* here. When we do entertain, it's the mayor and his family, or the Beauforts and Culverts. Not… teachers." She swallowed heavily and picked up her glass to take a long sip of wine.

Tommy, who'd been tidying away the dishes, snatched the glass from her, causing some of the red wine to spill onto the table and her dress. She stared down at the splash and mumbled an apology into her chest. "I didn't mean to offend."

While I knew Jack very well, I knew his cousin hardly at all. I wasn't even sure if she knew of my existence until quite recently. Whether she knew Jack had been my lover or not, I couldn't say.

"I'm not offended," I told her. "How can I be when you only spoke the truth?"

"That's not the point," Jack ground out.

"Nonsense. If I am not offended then you have no right to scold her on my behalf. She meant no harm by it, and I am not harmed. End of story."

Jack muttered something I couldn't hear under his breath. Hannah bit her lip and wisely stayed silent. She knew how Jack and I could clash on occasion, although seeing each other so rarely of late meant that our exchanges were usually more polite.

Samuel began to laugh. "So there is some fire in you, after all, Charity." He raised his glass to me. "I'm glad to see it."

My insides tensed at his words. Whereas Sylvia's slight had not hurt me in the least, his made me recoil. I knew it wasn't his intention. I knew he was trying to get me to relax, but that was the problem. *Why* did he want me to relax? Why did he want to be my friend?

Only a naive woman would not know the answer to that. And I was certainly not naive when it came to relations between men and women. He must think me a fool.

I liked him less and less.

Tommy handed Sylvia a cloth to wipe her skirt. She took it and dabbed at the splash, but it made no difference. The wine would leave a stain. She did not admonish him. Indeed, she seemed rather mollified by his impertinent action. That wasn't something I'd expected from the condescending Sylvia at all.

"Shall we retreat to the drawing room for a game of cribbage?" Hannah said, rising. "Will you join us, Tommy?"

Sylvia stiffened. "Really, Hannah? Can we not maintain some sort of order in front of our guest?"

"You said yourself that she's not our usual sort of guest. Besides, she and Tommy are friends, they have been for years. I'm sure they want to talk."

Sylvia's narrowed gaze slid to me. She scrunched the cloth up into a tight ball and shoved it into Tommy's chest. "I had forgotten how well they knew each other." She stalked out of the room.

I stared after her. She may not be able to start fires like Jack or hypnotize like Samuel, nor was she a genius like Langley or a mute like Bollard, but she was the oddest of them all.

***

The nightmares woke me. I lay on the bed and tried to breathe deeply to calm my frayed nerves, something I did most nights. I listened to the sounds of the night and was surprised to learn that the countryside was not as quiet as the city. In London, the occasional rumble of wheels could be heard, but mostly the dense fog smothered any noises. There were no owls announcing their presence, no insects or frogs providing a background rhythm.

After what seemed like an age of tossing and turning, I got up and threw a shawl around my shoulders. I lit a candle and checked the clock on the mantel. Three AM. Too early for the servants to be up preparing breakfast, but I was starving. Lying awake doing nothing made me hungry and I often raided Cook's pantry for bread and cheese back home. Hopefully the Frakingham cook would be as understanding.

I didn't know my way around the house, but I managed to find the service area after taking a few wrong turns. From there, it was easy to locate the kitchen and scullery. I was about to enter the pantry when I heard footsteps on the flagstone floor.

My breath caught in my throat and my heart ground to a halt. I couldn't move. Someone was coming and I would be caught in a place where I shouldn't be. I would be punished.

But that was a foolish notion; I was in a house among friends. The worst that could happen would be the cook becoming upset that I'd entered her domain uninvited.

I was wrong. The worst that could happen would be Samuel Gladstone appearing. He stood in the doorway, smiling. Always smiling. A small chill crept down my spine, but at least my heart restarted.

"It's you," he said. "I thought it might be Jack, checking on things."

I swallowed and forced myself to speak normally, as if I hadn't just received a fright. "He checks on things in the middle of the night?"

"Sometimes. He doesn't always sleep well after the events of a few months ago. Neither of us do."

"That makes three of us." I nodded at the pantry. "I was about to get something to eat."

"You should try the spiced biscuits, if there are any left over from afternoon tea. They're delicious."

"I will. Thank you."

I waited, but he did not leave. Instead, he came into the kitchen, his smile having disappeared. "Are you worried about the hypnosis? Is that why you can't sleep?"

"A little." It wasn't a lie. I was worried about it, but it wasn't the reason I couldn't sleep.

He set his candlestick down on the table and touched my arm. I shifted away before I realized what I was doing. His fingers curled into a fist then dropped to his side. "Sorry," he murmured.

I should tell him he had nothing to be sorry for, but I didn't. My insides knotted again.

He cleared his throat. "August Langley may be a little dramatic at times, but he's right. If you have any doubts about blocking your memories, then you shouldn't go through with it."

"I have thought it through."

He held up his hands in defense. "Of course you have. I didn't mean to imply you couldn't think, or… hell." He smiled again, somewhat sheepishly. "I'd better stop talking."

Mercifully. Perhaps he could stop smiling, too. He smiled far too often, there was just no need for it. What did he find so amusing? Me?

I clutched my shawl closed at my throat, covering myself up as best as I could, and wished I'd used a broach to clasp the two ends together. With the candle in one hand, the shawl in the other, I had no free hands. I had to wait for him to go if I wanted to forage through the pantry.

He didn't leave, not even after a long, strained silence. "I thought you could stay at Frakingham longer," he finally said. "Do you have to rush back to London so soon?"

"I have work at the school. The children need me."

"Yes, of course. They're important to you, aren't they?"

"Yes."

"As important as you are to them, I'm sure."

"I suppose." Why wouldn't he just leave?

"If there's anything you need, I hope you'll consider coming to me for help."

"Thank you. We have everything we need there. The Beauforts are generous benefactors."

He stepped closer—far too close—and I leaned back a little. "I meant you, Charity. If there's anything *you* need."

"There's nothing. The Beauforts pay my wages. As I said, they're generous people."

"I didn't mean financially." He cleared his throat. His cheeks seemed to redden a little, but it could have been the light from our candles playing tricks. "Unless that's what *you* mean." He cleared his throat. "Hell. What I meant was… anything. If you need anything at all, please come to me."

Ah, yes, *of course*. How stupid of me. He wasn't being kind, he was being vulgar because I was a loose woman. To him, I was nothing more than a mistress in need of a new benefactor. How base he must think me. How desperate. Horrid man.

"I won't be needing your help after tomorrow," I bit off.

He blinked. "Oh." The note of disappointment proved my assumption had been correct.

I tightened my hold on the heavy candlestick and edged past him.

"Where are you going?" he asked.

"That's none of your affair."

"I, uh... sorry. It's just that I thought you were hungry." He indicated the pantry.

"My appetite has vanished. Good night."

"Charity." His voice came from directly behind me, even though I'd walked swiftly to the door. I paused, in case he was going to grab me and stop me. It was best not to resist. "Have I upset you? My offer of help was innocently meant, but if I've wounded your pride, I'm sorry. It wasn't my intention."

Innocently meant?

"Indeed, I was hoping we could become friends."

"We can't." Perhaps he hadn't been asking me to become his mistress, but there was no way on this earth we could ever be friends. Not a man like him and a woman like me. Not only were our stations so far apart, but I didn't trust him. How could I, with his charming smiles, melodic voice and ability to hypnotize?

"Why not?" he asked.

"Because I don't like you." There. I said it. I peeked a glance at him through my lowered lashes. He stood there, staring at me, his eyes wide and unblinking. He looked quite shocked. He probably wasn't used to not being liked, particularly by a woman. He was a handsome man with impish dimples and bright, dancing eyes. How females must swoon when he bestowed a smile on them.

Not this female.

"Good night, Samuel." I strode out the door and did not look back. My stomach growled as I climbed back into bed and pulled the covers up to my chin. I stayed awake, replaying the conversation over and over, until I finally fell asleep at dawn.

***

"Let's be very clear," Samuel said. "You wish to forget the events leading up to the fire that gave you those scars, and only those events?"

I ignored the urge to tug on my sleeves to cover my hands and tilted my chin up. "Yes."

Samuel glanced at Jack. We sat in one of the smaller parlors that looked out onto the terraced garden. The door was closed and we were alone. I knew Hannah was reading in the drawing room not far away, Sylvia with her. Tommy had given me a reassuring smile as we passed in the hall. I'd not seen August Langley or his assistant all morning.

"I wish to remember everything else from my childhood and growing up," I told Samuel. "Even the memories that aren't so pleasant."

Jack took my hand in his. "I'm glad you want to remember our time together."

I squeezed his fingers. I wanted to say something profound about our special bond, but nothing came to mind. Having Samuel in the room with us made intimate discussion awkward. It made *me* awkward.

Samuel cleared his throat. "Ready?"

"Ready," I said. "Proceed, please."

I expected him to pull out the watch from his fob pocket and dangle it in front of my nose, but he merely sat back and pierced me with that penetrating gaze of his. Unease touched my consciousness, but it vanished almost immediately.

"Close your eyes, Charity," he intoned. "Listen to my voice." How could I not? It was beautiful, and so rich and deep that I wanted to sink into it. If voices were colors, his would be all of them, in every hue. "Show me the memories you want to forget. I'll keep them safe for you."

A moment of panic seized me. Even though I didn't want to stop his voice, I knew I *should* want to. Having so much power over another was wrong, dangerous. Frightening. But his continuous voice soothed my trembling nerves. It was like having a long piece of rope tied around my waist and he was pulling it, drawing me closer to him. When all the rope was gone, and lay puddled on the floor at our feet, he opened his arms and welcomed me into his warm embrace.

I lifted my face to gaze upon him. Beautiful, beautiful man. He continued to talk, but I didn't hear his words anymore, just the tone of his voice. It caressed me like a ribbon of soft light, stroking me piece by piece. It loosened the tightness in me, opened what had been shut, shone its light into the corners and chased away the shadows. It was the most wonderful, fulfilling experience of my life.

"My God." His gasped words were like a slap across my face.

The ribbon slid from my mind as if it had been yanked out. The invisible rope connecting us fell away. I felt like I was sliding backwards until I slammed into a wall.

The air was knocked out of me. I opened my eyes and Samuel stared back, his eyes huge, yet his mind's focus elsewhere. The orbs weren't so bright anymore either, more the dark, swirling blue-gray of an angry sea. He gripped the arms of his chair, his knuckles white. His chest rose and fell with every labored breath.

"Should she be awake yet?" That was Jack, who still held my hand.

I couldn't look at him, only at Samuel. Instinct told me to ask him what he'd seen to produce such a reaction, but I knew that was foolish. I'd wanted him to block my memories. And he had. I felt lighter, freer, yet there was a gaping hole in my past. It was what I'd expected, what I wanted.

Now I could move on.

"Thank you," I said to Samuel. "Thank you for helping me. It worked."

His eyes fluttered closed. When they reopened, they were more focused, although their normal color did not return. He passed his hand over his mouth. It shook. When he noticed, he stood abruptly and strode to the window, as rigid as a pole.

I had a desperate urge to go to him and wrap my arms around his waist. But, of course, I would not; ladies didn't do that sort of thing to gentlemen, no matter how much they desired them. I may not *be* a lady but, as a teacher, I had to keep up a respectable appearance and shun my past.

"So you recall why you're here?" Jack asked me.

"Of course. Samuel blocked some of my memories."

"And you don't remember which ones?"

"No. They're gone. There is only an empty space, now." I struggled to find the words to describe it. "I know they're missing. I know they must have been awful for me to want to remove them, but there's not even an echo of them. I have no inkling as to what they might have been."

"You recall everything else? Me, for example?" He paused and blew out a breath. "Us?"

"Yes, Jack, I remember us. I remember how we laughed and fought, and stole to survive. Those bad memories are still there, the good too. I remember when you went away and took Tommy with you. I remember trying to get work and failing. I remember becoming the… companion of a kind gentleman who educated me in a great many things."

I glanced at Samuel, but he didn't show any signs of shock. Of course he wouldn't. He knew what I'd done and what I'd been. I bit my lip and turned away. I couldn't look at him. What we'd shared was far more intimate than any relationship I'd had. I wasn't ashamed of the pieces of my life that I remembered, but I hadn't expected to feel so exposed. I forced myself to continue. The feelings would disappear once I left Frakingham and was away from Samuel.

"I remember when he died and I was set adrift for a time. I found work in a shop, then at a school. I wanted to be a governess or teacher. After that... nothing. My memory goes blank and returns again after our reunion, Jack. I remember your attempts to help me find work, but there are gaps there too, like a book with several missing pages. The next complete memories I have are of being a teacher at the orphanage."

Jack patted my hands, drawing attention to the scars there. They were horrible, puckered things that covered almost the entire backs of my hands and part of the front. I was about to ask him how I'd gotten them, but stopped myself. I drew my hands away and tucked them into the folds of my skirt.

"That's good," he said. "So it worked."

"It would seem so."

Samuel turned to look at me over his shoulder. His wild gaze connected with mine, sending a jolt through me. He quickly turned back to stare out the window. "So... you feel well?" he asked.

"Yes, thank you."

"You're smiling."

"Am I?" Indeed I was. I couldn't help it. Although I was troubled by the change in him, I was happier than I'd been in years. I felt normal. No more anxiety, no more self-loathing. I did feel somewhat self-consciousness, now that Samuel knew me like no one else did, but it was a small price to pay.

"I've never seen you smile," he said.

"Oh." It sounded pathetic, but his words struck me. Had I really never smiled during these last few years?

"I'm glad." He didn't sound glad, he sounded troubled.

I got up and went to him, but did not touch him. Instinct and concern propelled me that far, but propriety stopped me comforting him like I wanted to. "Samuel." Damnation. What could I say?

I didn't think you'd be so upset by something that happened to me.

I'm sorry I gave you my awful memories, but I don't want them back.

32

They weren't *his* memories. Whatever they were, he'd only seen them, not lived them. He would be well again, in time, once he'd locked them away. Something, apparently, which I'd failed to do. All I could do now was be his friend. He'd tried to be a friend to me since we'd first met, but I'd pushed him away. I didn't know why; I supposed my reluctance had something to do with my horrible memories. Yet, how could that be? If he'd been in any way connected, I wouldn't have come to him for help.

Ah well. It would remain a mystery. Those memories were gone and I didn't have to shun him anymore.

Despite my conviction that I should maintain distance, I touched his hand to offer support. A jolt shot through me. Images flashed before my eyes—the blue sky, trees and grass. A lake and some ruins visible in the distance. Good lord!

I leapt back, severing the connection. The strange vision ended. I was once more staring at Samuel.

He spun round. His lips parted, his brow furrowed. "Did you…?"

I pressed a hand to my waist and nodded. "I saw," I whispered.

"Saw what?" Jack asked, glancing from me to Samuel.

"I saw what he was looking at." I nodded at the window. "Out there. Samuel, did you see through my eyes?"

"No. I was on a busy London street."

"You saw through the eyes of another? Who?"

CHAPTER 3

"Charity?" Jack whispered. "What happened?"

I shrugged. "I don't know. It was like I was looking through Samuel's eyes."

"And I was looking through someone else's," Samuel said, without taking his gaze off me.

"Whose?" Jack asked.

Samuel rubbed his temple. "I don't know. I could only see what he or she saw. I'm sure it was London's Bond Street. There were coaches, horses, shopkeepers, people going about their daily lives, right in front of me. I felt like I was right there."

"Were you with someone?"

"I don't know. The vision was fleeting. I barely had enough time to register what I was looking at before it was gone."

I rubbed one of my scarred hands. "It happened when I touched you."

He tucked his own hands behind him, as if he were afraid I'd touch him again, or that he'd touch me.

"Has this ever happened when you have hypnotized someone before?" Jack asked, sounding concerned.

Samuel shook his head.

"Do you know what may have caused it this time?"

"No."

"Could it have something to do with the abrupt way the hypnosis ended?"

"I told you, I don't know!"

"Calm down, Gladstone. I'm simply trying to determine what happened."

"You think I want this?" Samuel growled. "You think I wanted to end the hypnosis like that?"

"Why did you?"

Samuel clamped his mouth shut so tightly I heard his back teeth grind. He stared at the rug.

Jack squared up to his friend. He looked as if he'd wrestle the answer out of Samuel, but then he suddenly backed down. He swallowed heavily and glanced at me out of the corner of his eye.

"They must have been shocking memories," I said quietly. My throat was swollen and tight. It was an effort to say that much.

Nobody said anything for some time. I wondered if Jack wanted to know what those memories were, but he didn't ask and I knew he wouldn't. Indeed, perhaps he already knew. I couldn't recall now.

"We'll find a way to control the visions," Jack said. "We can't have you two looking through other people's eyes, willy-nilly. Who knows what you might see?" He laughed uneasily.

"Don't concern yourself," Samuel sneered. He strode past us towards the door.

"Where are you going?" Jack called out.

"For a walk."

"Is that wise?"

"I can go for a bloody walk if I want to."

We watched him leave. He seemed to take some of the chilly air from the room with him. "Should I go after him?" Jack asked.

"Let him be alone for a while. Maybe he just needs time."

He sighed. "I've never seen him like this. He's always been so amiable, so easy to talk to. I know he has secrets and I've never pressured him to reveal them, but they don't seem to have affected him."

"Are you sure?" I sat again and smoothed my skirts flat across my lap. "I sensed some shadows in him, even before this. I didn't ask him about them, because I had enough of my own to contend with. I regret that now."

Jack sat opposite me and smiled. "That, in itself, is a good sign."

"What do you mean?"

"You've never given Samuel a second thought. You never seemed to care a whit for him and certainly never showed any regret at not getting to know him better. Indeed, you've always avoided him and I know that's troubled him, in the past. It would seem the memory block is working. Already it's unburdened you. The change in you is plain to see."

"I can feel it." I smiled, but it wasn't entirely sincere. I may have avoided Samuel in the past, but now that I wanted to get to know him better, he was avoiding me.

***

When Samuel hadn't returned by four o'clock, we grew worried. Even Mr. Langley sent Bollard into the drawing room to inquire if he'd returned. Twice. Watching the servant communicate with Jack was quite a curiosity. His hands and fingers moved swiftly, forming shapes and signs that seemed to mean something to the other members of the household. Jack didn't use hand signals to respond, though. Bollard was mute, not deaf.

He nodded, grim-faced. It was the first true expression I'd seen him make. The fellow had been quite vacant up until that point.

I waited for Bollard to leave before I made my suggestion. "I'll go in search of Samuel and bring him back."

"Don't be absurd," Sylvia said, snippy. "You're not familiar with the estate or the village. How will you know where to look?"

She had a point, yet I wanted to be the one to search. He'd done me a service and was suffering for it. "It's my fault that this has happened. What he saw when he hypnotized me has shocked him. I should be the one to find him and talk to him." Just saying it was difficult. How shocking could my memories have been to affect a man in such a way? I didn't want to think about it. Didn't want to know.

Sylvia resumed her sewing while Hannah and Jack exchanged worried glances.

"I'm leaving in the morning," I reminded them. "I want to depart as Samuel's friend. I want to know that he's all right."

"He'll be fine," Jack assured me.

"Samuel is very strong," Hannah said. "He was a great help when we went through our difficulties. Jack's right, Samuel will be himself again shortly."

"Nevertheless, I want to talk to him," I said.

"And say what?" Jack snapped.

"Jack," Hannah scolded.

"It's all right," I told her. Sometimes I thought she forgot that Jack and I had been close once. So close that we'd always spoken our minds to one another, even when what was on our mind was a sharp barb aimed to hurt. We'd grown up since then, thank goodness, but that directness between us had never quite gone away.

"You came here to remove the memories, Charity," Jack said. "You need at least *some* time without them."

"You think I'll ask him to remove the block?"

"You might," he hedged.

"Would that be a problem?"

"Hannah and I urged you to do it. Samuel too. We don't want you to go back. Not before you've been without them for a while. Samuel will be all right. We'll see to it."

"How? You're going away on your honeymoon, soon."

"I'll still be here," Sylvia said cheerfully. "Tommy, Uncle and I will keep a watchful eye on him."

"See," Jack said. "He's in good hands."

I eyed Sylvia as she embroidered a square of cloth. I wasn't so sure she was capable of taking care of a troubled Samuel, but her inclusion of Tommy eased my conscience. He was reliable and loyal. If Jack asked him to monitor Samuel, he would.

"Now, stop worrying," Jack told me. "Go back to your students and enjoy your new life."

I gave him a smile. "I will, thank you. But I still wish to help you look for him today."

He rolled his eyes. "Females. I suppose you want to come too, Hannah?"

She grinned. "Of course. I wouldn't want to miss an adventure. Besides, Samuel is a friend. I want to help him." Her good humor was infectious. She made me feel as if everything would work out well.

The three of us set off in the Langley growler. We peered out the windows and scoured the nearby countryside for signs of Samuel. Jack, however, was quite certain he'd gone into the village. We fell into an uneasy silence until I broke it when we arrived in Harborough.

"Do you know what happened to me?" I asked him. He sat beside Hannah, their hands linked on her knee. They were such a close couple, so perfect for one another. I hoped I could one day find my perfect husband too, now that I was free. "I can't recall if I told you."

He took a moment to answer. "I know a little," he finally said. "You told me some details, but not all of them. Just enough to…" He stopped himself with a sharp intake of breath. He turned to look out the window. "We're here."

I didn't push him. He'd said enough to answer my curiosity. It would seem Samuel was indeed the only person in possession of complete knowledge of my past. He was my memory keeper, and I felt compelled to ensure he was safe and well. I owed him that, at least.

The Red Lion was a large establishment on a prominent corner in Harborough. It was the favored inn of the village's heavy drinkers, Jack claimed. He and Samuel usually went elsewhere.

Most of the patrons looked up as we entered. Some nodded a greeting at Jack, but many did not. Their wary gazes followed our progress through the taproom to the lone figure sitting on a stool at the far end of the long polished bar. He was slumped forward a little, a glass of ale in his hand. A serving girl leaned against him, her bosom pressed into his arm. She spoke rapidly, stroking his blond hair. Samuel didn't seem to be listening. He propped his head up with one hand and stared into his glass.

"You won't find answers in there," Jack told him.

Samuel's gaze drifted to mine and narrowed. "You brought the heavy artillery, I see. You need not have bothered, I'm not finished here yet. Go away."

I was quite sure he was talking to me, or perhaps all three of us, but it was the serving girl who left, and not without flinging a scowl at me first.

"Come home," Hannah said. She touched his hand like I wanted to, but was too afraid. "Please, Samuel. We miss you."

He pressed the heel of his hand to his forehead, as if trying to suppress a headache. "Thank you," he muttered. "But I'm not ready to return."

"When then?"

"Tomorrow."

"After I've left," I murmured.

Samuel didn't answer, nor did he look at me. I folded my arms and hugged myself against the cold chill that swept down my spine. Hannah put her arm around me, but didn't refute my statement. We all knew it was true.

"Snap out of it, Gladstone," Jack growled. "You're making the ladies uneasy."

Samuel raised his glass in salute. "I'm terribly sorry, ladies. But if you don't mind, I need some peace and quiet." He pointed his glass at me. "You may not believe it, but this isn't about you."

I believed him. I knew enough from my days of living on the London streets, dodging the drunkards of both sexes to know that an excess of drink led to an excess of the truth.

"Then what is it about?" I challenged. "Why are you sitting here, drinking alone, staring morosely into your glass so soon after you hypnotized me?"

"I'm not alone." He nodded at the serving girl who'd been keeping him company. "Emily was here. Or was it Emma? Anne?" He shook his head. "My head hurts too much to think about names."

I forged on. "Forgive me, but I can't ignore the coincidence in the timing."

"Try harder."

I pressed my lips together to suppress the retort that sprang to mind. I needed to remember that he'd done me a service and was usually a good, kind man.

"Oh, Samuel," Hannah said on a sigh. "This isn't like you."

He swung round, splashing some of the ale over the sides of his glass. "How do you know? You met me mere months ago. None of you know the real Samuel Gladstone."

"Of course we do, dolt," Jack said. "You're a pompous toff, with more charm than one fellow has a right to have. Your constant smiling grates on my nerves and you have an annoying habit of bringing calm and reason to an argument. You make it impossible for anyone to stay angry with you for any length of time but, I can assure you, if you continue to refuse to come home with us now, I *will* get angry. In front of half the village. Is that what you want?"

He would do it, too. Jack wasn't one to back away from an argument.

"There are a lot of things that I don't want, Jack," Samuel said. "They happen anyway. Your still being here is one of them."

He did not move and I could see that Jack had run out of threats. Hannah took her husband's hand, as if she were worried he'd try to knock some sense into Samuel.

"Come on," Jack said to Hannah and me. "We can't help him if he doesn't want to be helped."

Hannah turned to leave, but I did not. I felt like Samuel was my responsibility now. We were linked through my memories and I was sure that it was those memories that had driven him to drink, despite his denial. Besides, I did not like the way he was treating two very good people.

I edged closer to him and leaned down so that only he could hear me. "For God's sake," I said between gritted teeth. "Your friends are worried about you. I'm worried about you. Come back with us."

The sinewy cords in his neck tensed, but he still refused to look at me. Indeed, he hadn't looked at me since he'd called me 'heavy artillery.'

"Go away, Charity," he said. "Go back to London. Our business is concluded. There's nothing to keep you at Frakingham."

Air escaped in a hiss through the gap in my teeth. Blood thudded between my ears. I pressed my palm flat on the bar beside his glass, but it did nothing to stem the rise of my anger. "You do not get to say when I go. I will not leave Frakingham until you've returned. Do you understand? So if you wish me to go home to London, then come back with us now. I'll keep to my original plan and be gone early in the morning."

He grunted a laugh. "So you're a stubborn female after all."

"And you're a toss-pot."

That produced a gasp from Hannah behind me and a chuckle from Jack. Samuel's jaw hardened. He twisted the glass slowly between both hands as he glared at it.

"I think I liked you better when you were reserved," was all he said.

"And I like you better when you're sober."

"Am I not charming enough for you now?" Finally he looked at me. My gut twisted at the sight of the wretchedness in his swirling blue-gray eyes and the twisted sneer on his lips. "And here I thought you loathed charming men."

"What do you mean?"

"Nothing," he mumbled, his gaze lowering.

I didn't press him. I had a feeling his accusation was linked to my memories.

"Samuel," Jack snapped. "You need to stop drinking before you say something you shouldn't."

"Drinking helps," Samuel said. "Believe me, it helps a great deal. You three leaving would help even more."

I'd had enough of his belligerence. Hannah and Jack didn't deserve it. I was quite sure I didn't either. Whatever memories I was now missing, I could still recall all of my conversations with Samuel. I'd been polite to him and not once had I led him to think I welcomed his attempts to court me. If I'd hurt his feelings then it was unintentional.

"Jack was right," I growled. "You're a toff, and a charming one at that. People like you, sometimes against their wishes. You've had an easy life because of it. Too easy. Perhaps that has blinded you to what a true friend looks like, but I can assure you that I can identify them when I see them. I ought to. I have so few. Jack and Hannah care for your wellbeing. To discount that is to hurt them. If you are any kind of a friend in return, you wouldn't want to cause them injury."

He was quiet for a long time. Not a single muscle in his face moved. I feared that I'd gone too far, but finally, he swallowed. "I see you found some of the fire I knew was in you," he said with a humorless smile.

"What's that supposed to mean?"

"Charity," Jack said. "Perhaps now isn't the right time."

"I want to hear what he has to say." The blood pumped through my veins. I was not usually so quick to rile, but I couldn't help it this time; he infuriated me.

"It means precisely that," Samuel said with a flourish of his hand in my direction. "You have a temper, Charity Evans, and where there's temper, there's passion and feeling.

Yet you've kept all of that locked away inside you. It would seem you've unlocked that door." He laughed. The brittle sound grated on my nerves. "It's my own fault, isn't it? I gave you the key and now you're unleashing your temper on me."

I pointed my finger at him. I knew I should feel some sympathy for him and perhaps guilt, but I was too angry to allow other emotions in. Besides, without knowing what memories I'd given him, it was difficult to fully understand his reaction. "Stop this. Listen to your friends. Come home."

"You're beautiful when you're angry. There. I can say it now. You're beautiful." He arched an eyebrow as if waiting for my response. "Ha. See, Jack? She's cured. She can now accept compliments and not recoil in horror at the poor fellow who pays them."

"Don't rile her, Samuel," Jack warned. "She's quite capable of making a scene."

Indeed I was. Every thud of my pulse was like a hammer blow to the shell that had encased me for so long. A shell I had no idea was even there, and now I had no idea *why* it was there, thanks to Samuel. How ironic that he would be the first to feel the force of my temper since the hypnosis.

"Do *not* change the subject," I spat. "Do not make jokes or pretend not to care." I stabbed my finger near his shoulder, pulling back before I touched him. "I will not leave here until you come with us, Samuel. I'll sit and drink alongside you until I am as drunk as you."

"Don't be a fool," he muttered.

"Why not? You are."

"Don't damage your reputation over this."

"You're damaging yours. Indeed, I have no reputation here. You do. Who is being the fool now?" I stabbed at him again, and this time I did not pull back. I connected with his shoulder.

My vision blurred. When it cleared, I couldn't see Samuel. I saw a room with books on large shelves, papers stacked neatly on a wide, deep desk, a silver inkwell nearby. A hand holding a pen stopped writing abruptly, breaking off mid-word. It was a man's hand. The fingernails were neatly trimmed and ink stained the middle finger. I had complete clarity as I looked down at the desk. No dizziness, no strange sensations of displacement or confusion. It was as if I were there in that room.

The vision vanished. I was staring once more at Samuel, and he stared back at me, his mouth open.

"What is it?" Hannah asked, gripping my shoulder. "Charity, are you all right?"

"Another vision," I murmured. "Samuel?"

He nodded. "I saw myself," he said. "I was standing where you are, looking through your eyes."

"Did you see through Samuel's eyes?" Jack asked me.

"No. I saw a study or office." I described the scene, including as much detail as I'd noticed. "It was a man's hand."

"Any clue as to who he was?"

"None. It wasn't a young man's hand, but it wasn't old, either." My earlier anger had vanished completely. I looked to Samuel and was surprised to notice that he seemed completely sober. He rubbed his chin in thought. "What's happening?" I asked him.

"I don't know. It's interesting that our visions have swapped. Last time, you saw what I saw and this time I saw through your eyes."

"Who is the third person? How is he connected to us?"

"I wonder..."

"What?" the three of us prompted.

"I wonder if it's Myer."

"Myer!" Everett Myer was another hypnotist. He was a strange man, oddly compelling yet quite morally skewed, according to Jack. He and Samuel were the only ones who could hypnotize people and block their memories. He was of middle-age and extraordinarily wealthy. "He's a banker, isn't he?"

"Not quite," Samuel said. "He has the principal share in his wife's family's bank, but I don't think he does any actual work for it."

"But it's likely that he has a study with a large desk in his London townhouse?"

"He does," Samuel said. "I've not seen inside it, though."

"It might be worth speaking to him about these visions," Jack suggested. "Even if it's not him, he might know why you're getting them."

"I don't like it," Hannah said. "That man is odd."

"I know," Jack said. "But he's the only one who may have answers."

"Do we need answers?" I asked. "I'm not particularly sure that it matters what we're seeing. It only happens when Samuel and I touch and that is unlikely to happen again."

He gave me a tight smile. "My charms continue to fail, I see."

I nodded at the empty glass. "I have no need for charms drowned in ale." Indeed I did not. I had the opportunity for a new, fresh start without my memories to burden me. I could be the woman I always wanted to be, have experiences I always wanted to have. I liked Samuel, liked him very much, but I would not be any man's amusement, no matter how rich or kind. I had done that before—the memory of the generous man who'd taken me as his mistress had not been erased. I had no need to go down that path now. I had the school and my students, I had money and a roof over my head, I had a future. If Samuel still wanted to court me then I would welcome it, but on my terms, not his. No doubt he would see pursuit wasn't worth it once he learned that.

I sighed. My thoughts had turned melancholy. I did like Samuel when he wasn't drinking. I hadn't realized how much until after the hypnosis. His charming manner no longer worried me, nor did the fact that he could hypnotize me, or anyone else, so easily. My feelings about that had changed. Although I could remember having felt that way mere hours earlier, I couldn't remember *why,* thanks to the memory block.

Part of me wished the circumstances were different and I could be something other than a mistress to him. But, of course, that could never happen, not with me being a less than virginal woman.

If Samuel understood my reservations, he gave no indication. Either our shared visions had sucked all the fight out of him, or my comment about drowning in ale had. Either way, he was quiet as we drove back to the house.

Sylvia and Tommy greeted us eagerly in the entrance hall. Even Bollard and Mr. Langley came to see how Samuel fared. He remained guarded in their presence, accepting their gentle admonishments with a shrug of his broad shoulders then excusing himself.

I followed him up the stairs. "Samuel, wait."

He paused on the top step and allowed me to catch up. He looked worn out and I was worried that I wouldn't see him at dinner. I needed to talk to him before I left, and I may not get another opportunity.

"There's no need to chastise me again," he said. "I know I upset my friends. It wasn't my intention."

"That wasn't why I wanted to speak to you. Samuel, I feel that I ought to apologize."

"Don't. And don't ask for the memory block to be removed either. It will change nothing. I told you, 'drowning my charms in ale' as you put it, is not entirely the result of what I saw in your memories. It's more to do with me."

Not entirely? "I... are you sure? You're not lying to me to ease my conscience?"

"No."

"It would seem this experience has changed us both. I suppose that was inevitable, in my case."

"But not in mine," he muttered.

"No."

We stood together in silence. The others had departed from the entrance hall below, leaving us alone. I suddenly felt shy again in Samuel's presence. He stared so intently at me, as if he could see into me. But that was absurd, he had no need. He'd already seen inside my mind. He knew me better than I knew myself. A blush crept up my throat and heated my face. I had to break the awkwardness cloaking us, yet part of me didn't want to. Part of me wanted him to kiss me.

"Samuel... if you need to talk to someone, please write to me. You say this is not my fault, but I am responsible, in a way. I won't let you suffer on my account."

"It's not suffering. It's... my cross to bear." He gave me one of his gentle, assured smiles, just like the old Samuel Gladstone. "I'll be back to myself, soon enough, well before Jack and Hannah leave, I'm sure. Stop worrying, Charity. But if it's all right with you, I will write. Perhaps I can even see you when I'm in London?"

I nodded, even though I knew I *should* refuse him. I should discourage his friendship and his advances. But I could not. If he needed me then I was obligated to help him, now. He was my memory keeper. In a way, he'd saved me by taking those memories from me. It was my duty to save him if he couldn't battle through his demons alone.

Besides, I *did* want to see him again. Very much.

CHAPTER 4

I awoke feeling more refreshed than I had in years. I'd slept through, without a single nightmare disturbing my slumber. It brought a smile to my face and a bounce to my step. Everyone noticed over breakfast. Everyone, that is, except Samuel. He wasn't there.

"He's still asleep," Tommy said, setting the teapot down on the sideboard.

"It's not like him to sleep late," Jack said.

"He was awake well into the early hours. I did my rounds, checking on the house, at about four and found him doing the same. He said he had not had a wink."

My good humor vanished. Poor Samuel. Not only had he gained my memories, I'd given him my nightmares, too. "If it's all right with you, Jack, I'll stay at Frakingham a little longer. Just until he's feeling better again."

"No," Jack and Hannah both said.

"The school needs you," Hannah added. "We know how you itch to be there again."

I did indeed. I'd not expected to miss the children so much, but I yearned to see their smiling faces again and feel their small arms wrapped around me.

Sylvia, sitting beside me, accepted a plate of bacon and eggs from Tommy. She was the only one he served. The rest of us served ourselves from the selection of dishes on the sideboard, as was the morning custom. Nobody raised so much as an eyebrow at the special treatment he gave her, but it got me wondering why her and not anyone else.

She picked up her teacup. "I do think it's best that you leave. You're something of a distraction."

"Sylvia!" Jack scolded.

She looked taken aback. "What is wrong with that? Isn't it nice to be a distraction for a man? I know *I* would take it as a compliment."

"Believe me, you're more than a distraction for some around here," Jack muttered. "You're a disruption of seismic proportions."

She pulled a childish face at him. "I don't know what seismic means, but I'll take it as a compliment."

"I don't think I distract Samuel *that* much," I told her gently. "Besides, what am I distracting him from?" Indeed, Samuel didn't seem to do much around Frakingham. Jack took care of the estate for his uncle, but Samuel had no function that I could see. For such an active man, it seemed odd.

"His work with Uncle, of course."

"Oh? What are they working on?"

She peeked over the cup rim at me. "This and that. I'm not really sure." She appealed to Jack.

He shrugged. "They won't say. Something to do with hypnotism."

A sinister thought struck me. "You don't think our shared visions have something to do with their experiments?"

Sylvia dropped her cup onto the saucer with a clatter. "I knew something like this would happen! I knew we couldn't be normal for long. Why does Uncle always do this? Why can't he work on normal drugs like normal microbiologists?"

"We don't know that for certain," Hannah said to me. She continued carefully, "It's a possibility, though. We shouldn't discount anything as the cause at this point."

Sylvia clicked her tongue. "I wish Uncle would leave well enough alone. Didn't he learn from the last time?"

"Not only August," Jack said, "but Samuel, too. Whatever they're doing, we must trust that it's harmless."

"If it were harmless," Tommy said quietly, "then why would they keep it a secret?"

Nobody had a response to that, although Sylvia did look irritated that the footman had spoken out of turn. She held out her teacup. "More tea, Tommy. Now."

"Ask me nicely, Miss Langley, and I will."

I bit my lip to stop my gasp. Was he mad? Did he want to lose his position? He ought to apologize immediately.

But it was Sylvia who backed down. She returned her teacup and saucer on the table, huffed, and pushed herself up. "The lack of respect in this household is astounding. Does no one believe in the proper order of things, anymore?" She tossed her head, lifted her chin, and stalked off.

Tommy bowed as she passed him. She paused, took one look at him as he straightened, a small smile playing on his lips, then stormed out in a swish of skirts.

***

I didn't see Samuel until I was about to step into Mr. Langley's coach for the drive to the station. My luggage was already secured to the back and Tommy held the door open for me with such stiff formality that I began to giggle. I wasn't sure I'd ever get used to seeing him in his role as footman. He'd been so mischievous when we were younger, and now he was so rigid. Indeed, he seemed even more rigid since Sylvia's scolding over breakfast. Poor Tommy. I got the feeling he was caught between trying to please the pretty, proud Miss Langley, and getting her to see him more as a man than a servant. I didn't know why he persisted; she didn't strike me as being particularly worthy of him.

At the urging of my friends, I'd decided that returning to London was best for everyone. Not only for the children and me, but for Samuel as well. Even Jack thought having me around could be affecting Samuel.

I was pleased to see him when he emerged from the house. He looked like his old self again, with his perfectly groomed hair and warm smile. But as he drew closer, I saw the bruised look to his eyes, the deeper lines around his mouth. He was tired, but he was putting on a brave face. For me.

I said my goodbyes and wished Jack and Hannah well on their upcoming journey. They both promised to write, but I rather expected they'd be too busy to think of me. Hannah's excitement at finally seeing more of the world was palpable. I was pleased for her and happy for Jack. Going by the way he gazed at his wife, he didn't care where he went, as long as she was by his side. It made my heart swell, not only for them, but for me, too. They made me believe that love did exist.

I kissed their cheeks, and that of Sylvia, too. Her polite smile turned to a scowl, however, when I embraced Tommy. I didn't care that he was a footman and she his master's niece. He was also my friend. Yesterday morning, before the hypnosis, I cared about doing the right thing. Today, not so much.

I stretched out my hand to Samuel, but quickly withdrew it. I gave him an apologetic smile. "We shouldn't."

He bowed. "Safe journey, Charity." He didn't promise to visit or write, and nor did I. It seemed best to avoid the topic altogether.

He stood to one side of the coach steps, Tommy on the other as I ascended. I turned to say a final "God speed," to Hannah and Jack, but the horses shifted at that moment. I lost my balance and flailed my arms in an attempt to grab hold of something solid. I did. Samuel.

He caught me round the waist and steadied me. My face was level with his. The dark swirl of his eyes sucked me into their depths and his breath warmed my lips, mere inches from his own.

And then he was gone.

My vision blurred then cleared to reveal a bustling city street filled with men walking along the footpath. Crowded omnibuses rattled by, also filled with men. It was early in the morning, so I assumed they were probably heading to work in the stately buildings on either side of the street. The man whose eyes I was looking through had been walking, but he'd stopped when I entered his vision. I knew this because I—he, we?—looked down and saw his feet and the end of a black cane.

A violent shiver wracked me. My stomach rolled and, for a moment, I thought I'd throw up. I covered my mouth with my hand and once more found that I was back inside my own body, staring directly at Samuel. We were no longer touching.

"Are you all right?" he asked, frowning. "You're very pale."

"As are you."

He did indeed look as ill as I felt. His eyes were a fathomless whirlpool, their color bleak against the unnatural pall of his skin.

"Are *you* all right, Samuel?" I asked.

His eyes shuttered. He stepped back and dragged a shaking hand through his hair as he swore under his breath.

"What happened?" Jack asked. I hadn't seen him or the others draw close. Tommy now held me by the elbow, steadying me. It was just as well, as my legs felt like jelly. "Another vision?"

I nodded. "This one... it... disturbed me more than the others, but..." I sighed. "I don't know why."

Samuel's shoulders jerked as if he'd flinched. No one else seemed to have noticed how affected he was by the vision. They were all concerned about me. I desperately wanted to speak to him about it, and ask his opinion on the feelings I'd felt during it. The feelings I suspected he'd also felt.

But I did not.

Indeed, I didn't really know what to do. Comfort him? Stay longer and discuss it? Or leave, and do my best to forget? Were the visions linked to the memories I'd had erased?

It was a possibility, and because of that possibility, I wasn't willing to explore the vision further. The sooner I got away from Samuel and the potential to experience more visions, the better.

Tommy helped me into the cabin and the driver urged the horses forward. I resisted looking through the window, although I desperately wanted to see who watched me go. Or rather, if Samuel watched.

I gave in just before we reached the curve in the drive and glanced out the rear window. Jack, Hannah and Tommy stood where I'd left them, waving. Sylvia had turned and walked up the front steps. Samuel was nowhere to be seen and my heart dipped a little.

I was about to turn around to face the front when a movement at a second floor window caught my eye. I squinted and tried to fathom what I was looking at. Or rather, who. The blond hair was a giveaway. Samuel. He must have raced up there as soon as I left. He wasn't alone, however. Beside him, Mr. August Langley sat, and behind him stood Bollard. All three watched me drive off. They were too far away for me to read their expressions, but an uneasy feeling clawed at my gut. What interest could Langley possibly have in me?

***

"The Burcotts' ball was the most tedious affair I've been to since my return to England," said Cara Moreau with a grimace. She sat on the sofa in the school's drawing room and I sat opposite. It was the afternoon of the day after my return from Frakingham, and I'd been glad when she called upon me. Her friendly presence was always welcome and I'd been toying with the idea of talking to her about my visions.

"There were twice as many ladies as gentlemen and not nearly enough refreshments for everyone," she went on. "The ballroom was no bigger than this room."

We both glanced around the drawing room. It was as comfortable and welcoming as I could make it. It was almost a year ago when I'd been tasked by Mrs. Emily Beaufort, my patroness and Cara's niece, to make it a more inviting room. I'd filled it with framed artwork, painted by our more talented pupils, and relegated the stuffy portraits of previous headmasters to the long corridor. The sofa had been in Mrs. Beaufort's house before she redecorated, but most of the other furniture was made by our older students.

I leaned forward in my chair, keen to hear more. Cara loathed attending society's entertainments, but I enjoyed listening to her descriptions on her weekly visits. Newly returned from the wild Antipodean colony of Victoria, she had rather a unique perspective on the round of entertainments she was forced to endure in England in order to secure a suitable husband. Usually her descriptions involved the words pompous, shallow and limp. I pitied the poor gentlemen on occasion, but she did make them sound weak compared to the men she'd known in Melbourne.

"Did you dance?" I asked her.

"Unfortunately I had to endure several sets. The gentlemen were the dullest yet. Not a single one of them held me firmly. It's as if they thought I'd break."

"It's not entirely their fault," I said. "You do look fragile."

She rolled her eyes. "You sound like Emily."

"Perhaps she's despairing that you've not liked a single one of the gentlemen she's presented to you." I wouldn't normally dare speak to anyone so boldly, let alone my patroness's aunt, but I was feeling bolder. Besides, Cara and I were friends now. For some reason she'd taken to me instantly. Perhaps it was because we'd both lived on the streets as motherless children. Our early childhoods were remarkably alike, although she'd been taken in at the age of ten, by her newly discovered family, and I had not been so fortunate.

"I don't like them because the gentlemen are dull at best and vain at worst," she said. "Some are both. One fellow in particular proceeded to tell me about all the girls he'd danced with that evening and how not a one of them was up to his standard. They were too tall or too freckly, too fat or too thin, too simpering or too aloof. Can you believe it! What woman in her right mind would want to spend the rest of her life trapped in a marriage with that man?"

"What did you do?"

"I stood on his toe. Hard. I'm sure he told the next girl he danced with about the dusky-skinned girl's lack of grace."

We both giggled at that. "I'm sure it can't be all bad."

"True. It could be worse. There could have been ghosts there."

Cara was a spirit medium. She and her niece could both see and speak to ghosts as if they were living people. I'd been disconcerted by it at first, but quickly came to realize they were normal in every other way.

"Speaking of which," I said. "Have you met any handsome ghosts lately?"

"Dead men are not handsome, Charity. Their corpses are rotting away underground. Small creatures are making homes in their skulls."

I threw my head back and laughed. "How can you joke about such gruesome things?"

"How can you laugh at them?" She grinned. "It's good to see you laugh with such abandon. I never thought I'd see the day."

"Don't be silly. You often make me laugh."

She shook her head. "You've politely tittered, but never laughed. As your friend, I feel compelled to point out the change in you. I suppose it has something to do with that handsome Samuel Gladstone. Now *there* is a gentleman who could not be accused of vanity, even though he has every right to be vain with eyes that blue and the face of Adonis."

"Cara! He is not *that* handsome. He is certainly charming, I'll agree with you there." I frowned. "Usually."

"What do you mean? Was he rude to you? If he was, I'll have to go to Freak House and box his ears."

I smiled. "I'd like to see you try. He looks strong."

Her lips slowly spread into a smile. "He does indeed."

My face heated and I looked away. I wasn't prepared to discuss my attraction to Samuel with anyone. I wasn't even prepared to *think* about it.

Cara cleared her throat. "I'm sorry," she muttered. "I didn't mean to make you feel uncomfortable."

"Don't be. Samuel is… a nice gentleman. You ought to consider him as a suitor."

"I don't think I'm Samuel's type."

"Oh? What makes you say that?"

She blinked at me. "Instinct," she added quickly. "If I were his type, he'd have tried to court me already."

My heart did a little flutter. "He hasn't?" I tried not to sound pleased about it, but I think I failed. She gave me a sly smile.

"I danced with him once. It was pleasant, if uneventful."

"You mean you had no need to step on his toes?"

She laughed. "I mean there was no connection between us. No spark. Nothing. I do expect a spark, don't you?"

"I'm not sure. I agree there does need to be a sign, something clear that cannot be mistaken for mere friendship."

"Like a large diamond ring?"

We both fell about laughing in the most unladylike manner. It felt good to laugh with her. Utterly liberating. She was right, I hadn't laughed like that in… well, perhaps ever.

"I see the hypnosis worked," Cara finally said when our giggles subsided. "The change in you since your return is remarkable." She got up and took my hand in hers. "I'm so pleased to see it. I knew you could be like this. I knew it." She bent and kissed my cheek. When she pulled away, her eyes shone with unshed tears.

I didn't know what to say. She was right. I *was* happier. But to admit it was to acknowledge that something in my past had troubled me so much that it had altered my personality, destroyed the light in me, and filled me with darkness and fear.

I didn't want to give voice to that. The memory was gone. I did not want it back, not even the ghost of it.

There was no chance to discuss it further. A scream had me jumping to my feet and my heart leaping into my throat. Cara and I ran out of the drawing room and up the corridor in the direction from which it had come.

"Miss Charity! Miss Charity!" Little Charlotte, a six year-old orphan in my care, barreled down the passageway towards us, her pigtails flying behind her. "Miss Charity, come quick!"

"What is it?"

"It's Polly. She cut herself and there's blood everywhere!" She pulled a face. "I think she cut her leg off."

"Where is she?"

"Kitchen class, miss."

"What were you two doing in there unsupervised?" Another wail had me dismissing my own question. "Never mind. Charlotte, fetch Mrs. Peeble and ask her to bring bandages. And have her send for the doctor."

She raced along the corridor while Cara and I continued towards the kitchen classroom. Little Polly sat on the floor in a flood of tears, near one of the large tables, her skirt and petticoat pulled up to her knees. Blood oozed from a gash in her leg. The culprit—a long knife—lay beside her.

She sobbed upon seeing me. "It hurts, miss."

"I know it does, Polly. Let me see." I knelt and checked the wound. It was indeed long, but thankfully not deep. "The doctor will come soon and make it better."

"But it hurts *now*." Her face crumpled and she let out an almighty wail.

I drew her onto my lap and enclosed her in my arms. She nuzzled into my throat and buried her hands in my skirts.

Her blood smeared my clothes, but I didn't care. I just wanted to comfort her and stop her shaking. The warm little body was as much a comfort to me as I was to her. It felt good to embrace her, to be the center of her world, to be the one she needed.

I closed my eyes against a wave of emotion that rippled through me, but it didn't stop. My heart swelled. My pulse thudded. Tears came close.

A commotion at the door had me reopening my eyes. Charlotte and Mrs. Peeble rushed in, but it was Cara that caught my attention. She stared at me, her face soft, her eyes wistful. I'd forgotten she was there.

Mrs. Peeble set about cleaning the wound while I held Polly. She was a stout woman of about forty with broad, masculine features and hands. She wasn't gentle, but little Polly bore the teacher's ministration bravely.

"You girls shouldn't be in here alone," Mrs. Peeble scolded. "There are all sorts of things that could harm two naughty children."

"We only wanted to cut Dolly's hair," Charlotte said with a sniff.

"I want Dolly," Polly said, her lip wobbling. She pointed at a doll lying on the floor under the table.

Cara fetched it and the knife. She returned the knife to the table and gave the doll to Polly. The little girl tucked it between her body and mine.

Mrs. Peeble clicked her tongue. "The rules are clear. No one is allowed in the kitchen classroom without a teacher. You girls are old enough to know."

"It's all right, Mrs. Peeble," I said gently. "I think the girls have learned the hard way that knives can be dangerous."

"Ow!" Polly jumped as Mrs. Peeble began to wrap a bandage around the cut.

I tightened my grasp on her and she nestled against me once more. I kissed the top of her head and held her until Mrs. Peeble finished.

"That'll suffice until Dr. Cumberland can get here," Mrs. Peeble declared. "Off you go to class, girls."

Cara helped Polly to stand and then held her hand out to me. She was smiling curiously. Mrs. Peeble left, muttering about naughty children, and I sent the girls on their way.

"Try to stay seated as much as possible," I told Polly. "No running around for you today."

She threw her arms around me and hugged me with far more ferocity than I thought her capable of. "I love you, Miss Charity."

My throat closed. "I love you too, Polly," I managed.

She gave me a squeeze then ran after her friend.

"I said no running!" I called after her.

She slowed to a fast walk.

I smiled. "She'll be all right," I said to Cara. "But she certainly gave me a fright."

"So I saw." Cara made for the door in a swish of skirts. "I must go. You've got work to do and Emily has more torture in store for me this evening. I must try to tame this tangled mop into something presentable beforehand."

"Your hair is lovely," I assured her. "You're lovely. Enjoy your evening and be kind to the poor gentlemen who only wish to speak to a charming young lady."

"I will try, Charity, but if they turn out to be stupid or vain, I cannot promise not to step on their toes."

"I think that's entirely fair."

We chatted as I walked her to the front door, but I wasn't really listening. I couldn't stop wondering if Polly was resting her leg. Had it started bleeding again?

"Charity." Cara's curious tone caught my attention. She stopped near the coat stand and I stopped alongside her. "Forgive me for saying this, but… you've never held one of the children like that before, have you?"

The lump that had swelled in my throat when I held Polly formed again. I tried to shrug off her observation, but I couldn't be so glib. She was right, I hadn't. I shook my head but did not answer.

She touched my hand. Her thumb rubbed the scar. "I'm very glad."

I didn't ask her what she meant, although I suspected I already knew the answer. She was glad that my bad memories were gone, glad that I'd changed. Glad that I was now capable of giving affection to the children like I'd always wanted. I could finally love them the way they needed to be loved.

"So am I," I told her. "So am I."

***

It was late when I finally returned to my bedroom. I was tired and looking forward to a full night's rest. It would be my third without the nightmares. The prospect was deeply satisfying.

I undressed and reached around to my back, to scratch an itch that had been irritating me for the last half hour. My fingers touched roughened skin just below my shoulder blade. I twisted to see my back in the dressing table mirror. What I saw had me gasping in horror.

Several scars marred the skin. They were different to the ones on my hands, mostly long and thin, with some round ones overlapping.

My legs weakened. I plopped down on the floor and sucked in deep breaths. I had not known about them. They didn't hurt, but by the look of them, they once had. How had I got them?

I knew that answer. At least, I knew that the scars were linked to my missing memories. It would seem I couldn't escape the physical damage inflicted upon me as easily as the mental.

I didn't have time to contemplate it further. My vision suddenly blurred, in that now familiar but disconcerting way. When it cleared, it was as if I were standing inside a bedroom. It was a large bedroom with dark green and cream striped wallpaper, a heavy black mantel and sturdy four-poster bed. A young woman sat on the bed, dressed only in a chemise. She hugged her drawn-up knees and peered back at me through wet lashes.

Then the vision disappeared and I was once more in my own bedroom. I reached for my shawl and wrapped it around myself. My hands shook. My mind reeled.

Why had I experienced a vision now, when Samuel wasn't near? Who was the girl? And why did she look so frightened?

CHAPTER 5

It was some time before the effects of the vision wore off. It shook me to the core. Not only the fact that I'd experienced it without Samuel, but also because of the woman. Who was she and why was she crying? It was clear that I'd intruded on someone's intimate encounter in the bedroom.

Which meant someone had intruded on mine. I'd been naked. Thank goodness I hadn't been looking into a mirror at the time!

Everything was so confusing. Why was I experiencing a vision *now*? Why without Samuel?

I removed the shawl and stood, catching sight of my back in the mirror again. There were perhaps a dozen scars in all. I didn't know what could have caused the small circular ones, but I guessed the long ones to be from a whip or belt. That meant someone had inflicted them upon me, they had not been caused by accident.

My stomach rolled. Bile surged to my throat, burning and foul. I felt dizzy and had to sit again lest I fall.

Don't think, Charity. Don't give the scars another thought.

I couldn't see them very easily, so I could ignore them. They were a part of my forgotten past and that's where those memories must remain: forgotten.

I put on a clean nightgown and crawled into bed. I would *not* think about them again.

***

I received no more visions for the rest of the week. My life at the school felt blessedly normal. No, not quite normal... fulfilling. I hugged the children and they responded with affection. Somehow, those small gestures deepened my bond with them. It was like nothing I'd ever experienced before. I thought I'd loved my little orphan family of Jack, Tommy and the others, but this was different; there were no conditions placed upon it, no *need* for anything in return. A smile was enough, although they gave me much more. It was like their little arms circled my heart as well as my body, and remained there long after they'd run off to their next class. I found myself smiling during the day for no particular reason.

The nights were different. I would remain in their dormitory, reading or talking, until they fell asleep then leave them to the care of the matron and return to my own room. I would sit alone on my bed and avoid the mirror. For one thing, I didn't want to be caught looking at myself if I had a vision and, for another, I didn't want to give in to the compulsion to check the scars on my back.

I received a letter from Jack and Hannah. It was sent from Dover, on the morning they embarked on their honeymoon voyage to the continent. It was dated the day prior, so the ship would already have left. I felt a little less happy for them than I should have. It was more a sense of unease that Jack was no longer in England. He had always been there for me and I had always known where to find him if I'd ever needed him. Not that I had, but I'd not realized how secure that knowledge had made me feel until now.

I received another letter the following day from Samuel, asking me to meet with him. I considered refusing. Not only because we'd parted on awkward terms, but because he'd suggested we meet at Hyde Park, where the well-to-do liked to promenade. I didn't belong in such a place. I would be a weed among flowers, noticeable for all the wrong reasons.

On the other hand, I needed to discuss the last vision with him. Perhaps he had some insight into it, and I was curious if he'd experienced it too.

Yet the real reason I wanted to see him was simply that I *wanted* to. Against my better judgment, I liked his charming manners and smiling eyes. I was quite sure I could keep our acquaintance on a friendship basis only, though, as the alternative—being his mistress—was simply not an option for me, anymore.

In the end, after much contemplation of the issue, I decided to meet him. We were bound by my memories, and I couldn't abandon him if he needed me. Hopefully this meeting would prove that he was quite recovered and we could go our separate ways.

Cara came to my rescue after I lamented that I had nothing pretty to wear to the park. She loaned me a neat little military style jacket in peacock blue, and a matching hat and parasol. I couldn't borrow an entire dress from her, since she was shorter than me, but the accessories worked well with the dark colors of my wardrobe. Indeed, surveying my small collection of clothes made me realize how limiting the black and gray were. I should spend some of my savings and have something prettier made up.

Samuel had offered to pick me up, but I'd written and advised him that I'd meet him at the Hyde Park Corner entrance. That way we would be in a crowded place and not alone in a carriage.

I arrived early, but he was already there, leaning against the Wellington Arch as if he owned it. He pushed off from the stone structure upon seeing me and took my hand, bowing over it. If he thought it curious that my sleeves were shorter and no longer covered my scars, he didn't show it.

"I'm glad you came," he said, straightening. I got my first proper glimpse of his face. The shadows along his jawline could be attributed to not having a valet or barber handy, but not the shadows that hollowed out his cheeks or underscored his eyes. His eyes too still swirled dark and stormy, but the whites now sported spidery, red lines. My heart sank a little at the haggard sight of him. It sank even further when I drew close enough to smell the whiskey on his breath.

"How are you, Samuel?" I blurted out.

His lips curled into a sneer. "Why do you ask?"

I stepped back. His vehemence surprised me. "I… that is, it's the polite thing to ask an acquaintance."

He looked away and drew in a breath. When he turned back to face me, he was smiling, but it was a little too hard to be genuine. "Yes. Of course, my apologies. I'm well. And you?"

"In good health and spirits."

"I'm pleased to hear it." The smile turned soft, genuine. "Very pleased."

"Shall we walk? It's a pleasant day."

"It is? Perhaps underneath the gray pall."

I laughed. His own smile broadened. "You've been in Hertfordshire for too long. You've forgotten what it's like in London."

"Perhaps."

We set off along the gravel drive, keeping out of the way of other visitors. The park's roads were a veritable thoroughfare for young men driving their springy chariots at dizzying speeds to impress their passengers, and riders of both sexes on horseback. A little sunshine brought out the winter-weary Londoners like spring's first blooms attract bees.

"How is everyone at Frakingham?" I asked.

"Well enough, although the house is quiet without Jack and Hannah. I do wish Sylvia and Tommy would stop dancing around each other. It makes for a strained household."

I stopped and stared at him. "Sylvia and Tommy? So I wasn't imagining it?"

"Tommy likes Sylvia. Or she likes him. Perhaps. It's complicated and I don't think either of them knows what they feel."

How remarkable, and deliciously scandalous too. It explained a lot about the odd behavior I'd observed. "Does her uncle know?"

"Good lord, no. He'd put an end to it immediately, if he did. He would never agree to his niece being courted by one of the servants."

"The gap between them is rather wide," I mumbled.

"Cavernous. It would take a great love to close it and I'm not sure Sylvia has it in her to love on that scale. She's rather fickle."

"Tommy does. He's most steadfast."

His gaze slid to mine. "He's a good man."

"One of the best. He and Jack."

His jaw hardened. "Jack's gone for several months. Tommy's busy in Hertfordshire."

Why did he sound so irritated? What had I said? "And?"

"And I'm afraid you only have me."

"Afraid? Who for? You or me?"

He barked a short, harsh laugh. "I'm in earnest, Charity. If there's anything you need, you should come to me."

"Thank you, Samuel. It's very kind of you. I'd like to extend the same offer to you, too." I swallowed and looked down at my boots. I hoped he didn't think I was implying something improper.

"Actually, there is something. You can come with me to Everett Myer's residence."

"Myer! Why?"

"To question him."

"Can you not do it alone? I want nothing to do with that man."

He put his hands behind his back, linking the fingers tightly together. "Why?"

"Because he's... he's not someone I like very much."

He gave a harsh grunt. "Because he's a hypnotist, like me. Is that it?"

I was walking a delicate line and I needed to be careful not to stray too far to the left or right. "He unnerves me. It's hard to explain. It's more of an intuitive response than anything tangible."

"Ah, I see."

I did not like his sneering tone, nor did I think it fair that he directed it at me. "We're discussing Mr. Myer, Samuel, not you."

"We're the same."

"You are *not* the same."

"We're both hypnotists."

"Hannah and Jack were both fire starters, but they weren't the same."

"Semantics."

I huffed out a breath. The man could be so exasperating! It was most definitely a new development. He'd never been so difficult before. Indeed, he'd always said the right thing, as if he were incapable of offending anyone.

"Samuel, are we destined to argue about everything, now?"

He said nothing. He walked stiffly on, as if I'd not spoken.

"If this is the result of you keeping my memories then I'm not sure I like it so much anymore."

He stopped abruptly and blinked at me. The wretched mask he'd been wearing slipped off and I caught a glimpse of the friendly man I'd liked without even knowing that I'd like him. "I agree, Charity." He spoke quietly, as if afraid to frighten off a bird that had landed on the grass nearby. "I don't want to argue with you. I'm sorry. I'm… not myself, lately." He squeezed the bridge of his nose.

"I know. Because of—"

"Don't. We've been through this, and it is not because of you. If I hear you say that again I'll… throw myself in the Serpentine."

"Can you swim?"

"Yes."

"Then that is hardly a threat."

"It is if I emerge all wet."

Still not a threat, but I didn't admit that I would rather like to see him dripping wet, his shirt clinging to his chest.

"I'll dog your steps across London, telling everyone how I threw myself into the lake to prove a point to you," he said. "I'll gain all their sympathies and you'll be painted as the heartless shrew who forced me to do something drastic."

I laughed. The conversation had taken a silly turn, but it was good to see Samuel back to telling jokes and trying to make me smile.

He put his elbow out for me to take then let it drop with a sigh. "The visions. Well then? Will you come with me to see Myer? I thought we could ask to see his study and you can compare it to the one in your vision."

"If you'd said that before, we need not have argued in the first place. It's a very reasonable request. I had another vision too. Did you?"

"Yes." He said nothing further. If he had indeed seen my bedroom, it was gentlemanly of him not to mention it.

"There was a girl this time, sitting on a bed crying. Do you, uh, know who she might be?" I couldn't look at him. It was far too personal a question, but I needed to know that the girl wasn't crying because of *him*. I wasn't sure why that need was so strong in me, it just was.

Curiously, he did not seem either shocked or disturbed by my question. "No. I can assure you I haven't seen any girls sitting on beds in the last week, let alone tearful ones. She must have been with him."

"Yes," I said quietly. "I wonder why she was sad. Sad and frightened."

His Adam's apple jerked up and down. "I have no idea, but let's confront Myer. Hopefully he can provide answers."

***

Mrs. Myer didn't like me. I didn't need to have supernatural powers to know that the curve of her lips was more a smirk than a smile. Her critical gaze took in my face, figure and clothing—twice—and she didn't seem at all concerned that I might be embarrassed by her scrutiny. Indeed, she made me feel like a bolt of cloth in a draper's shop, the way she took my measure. I couldn't be sure if I met with her approval or not.

The false smile was soon turned on Samuel. "It's a pleasure to see you again, Mr. Gladstone," she said smoothly.

"Thank you, Mrs. Myer." The two exchanged pleasantries as I sat on the sofa in the Myers' drawing room and wondered what to make of her. She was certainly not the sort of wife I expected Myer to have. I'd met him briefly at the Beauforts' Christmas ball, and had found him to be charming and a little flirtatious. It was why I hadn't liked him then, just as I'd not liked Samuel. I was prepared to see him through different eyes this time, albeit guarded ones, knowing what role he'd played in Hannah's recent troubles.

His flirtatiousness with the prettier women at the ball had led me to think his wife would be pretty, but not even at my kindest could I call her that. She was plain and rather flat and broad, in both figure and face. I'd seen plainer girls overcome worse, but what made Mrs. Myer's appearance so unfortunate was the lack of spark in her eyes and her manner. The penetrating scrutiny and grim set to her mouth equated to a rather unhappy countenance. Ordinarily, I would have felt sorry for someone who seemed so unhappy, but instead I felt a little angry. She had enormous wealth at her disposal. She could afford to surround herself in luxury and immerse herself with entertainments or idle outings. If she preferred more cerebral stimulation then she could buy as many books as she wished, or if she had a kind heart then there were boundless opportunities for philanthropy. She was far more fortunate than the majority of people in London, yet she seemed like one of the most miserable I'd ever met.

I was prepared to concede that I'd judged too harshly and too soon, but as I watched her answer Samuel's polite questions with simple answers and not inquire about him in return, I didn't think I had.

Thankfully, her husband joined us before the conversation ground to a halt. "Ah, Gladstone, my dear fellow. What a pleasure to see you again." He shook Samuel's hand then bowed to me. "It's Miss Charity Evans, is it not?"

I nodded. "Hello again, Mr. Myer. I'm surprised you remembered me, we only met the once."

"I remember everyone I meet, especially ladies as, uh, memorable as you, my dear." Ordinarily such a sugary sentiment would have me recoiling at worst, or rolling my eyes at best. But it was so kindly said, and accompanied with such a warm smile, that I smiled back.

"Thank you, Mr. Myer. It's indeed a pleasure to see you again."

I caught sight of both Mrs. Myer and Samuel scowling, but not at me. At Myer. Had he just hypnotized me? Or simply charmed me? Good lord, surely it was the latter and not the former?

From what I knew of him, it wouldn't surprise me if he *had* hypnotized me. He'd tried to hypnotize Hannah, Samuel and Jack before he knew that both the men were immune. He'd then gone on to hypnotize his wife to remove her from the room. Despite his reservations, Samuel had spent some time in Myer's company, with the aim of studying their mutual ability. He'd given up on the scheme after Myer proved unscrupulous in his quest to learn as much about the supernatural as possible. None of the Frakingham residents liked him or trusted him, as it would seem he'd helped the man who'd kidnapped and tried to kill Hannah, but all conceded that he was needed from time to time.

"My dear, if you wouldn't mind leaving us," Mr. Myer said to his wife. "I'm sure you don't wish to hear us discuss business."

"Of course I do," she snapped. "Besides, it's not business they're here to discuss and you know it." The defiant gleam in her eyes was tantamount to a declaration of war. There was no marital bliss between this husband and wife.

"You leave me little choice," he told her.

"Myer!" Samuel's voice cut through the air like a sharp blade. "Do not hypnotize her."

"My dear fellow," Myer drawled. "I was simply going to ask her to organize tea since she insists on gracing us with her presence."

"It's too late for tea," she said. "Do you drink sherry, Miss Evans?"

"Not for me, thank you."

"A teetotaler, eh?" Myer chuckled. "How quaint."

I gritted my teeth. I did not bother to tell him that I didn't abstain from drink, I just didn't feel like it at that moment. I needed to keep my wits about me in the presence of this couple.

"Gladstone looks in need of a glass of whiskey," Myer said to his wife. "See to it."

She got up with a huff and strode to the bell pull then returned to her seat. "Proceed, Mr. Gladstone. What is it you and Miss Evans wish to speak to my husband about?"

"Visions," Samuel said. "We've both been having visions after I placed a block on some of her memories."

"*You* blocked some of her memories?" Myer slapped the palm of his hand down on the arm of his chair. "And this after you chastised me for the one I placed on Hannah Smith."

Samuel bristled beside me on the sofa. I could feel the tension pulsing off him. "Hannah was a child!"

"I requested it," I said before tempers flared further. "I was fully aware of what I would be losing." And gaining.

"Mr. Gladstone is right," Mrs. Myer said. "They're two entirely different things. I think Mr. Gladstone has already established himself as an upstanding young gentleman. *He* wouldn't hypnotize a young lady if it wasn't in her best interests."

Myer spluttered a laugh. "You ought not make such broad, sweeping statements, my dear. You cannot know a man well after a few brief encounters."

Samuel's hands, resting on his knees, curled into fists. He stared down at them, but did not argue the point with our host. It was most odd. Why didn't he defend his character?

"*I've* had more than a few brief encounters with him," I said. "And I *can* make such sweeping statements. Samuel only did what I asked of him. Jack Langley was there and observed the session."

"If you trusted Gladstone so implicitly, why did you need Langley there at all?"

I bit my lip, lest I say something I regretted, like calling him a foul name I'd frequently used as a child on the street.

Mrs. Myer had been watching the exchange with interest. Now her gaze settled on Samuel's. I suspected she was about to ask him something, but a footman entered. He listened to her instructions then left.

"Something strange happened, immediately after the block was placed on me," I went on before she could speak. I told them about the first vision, then the subsequent ones, and how we'd seen through each other's eyes and those of another man. "The first three times it happened when we touched. This last time, Samuel was in Hertfordshire and I was here, in London."

"Interesting," Myer murmured, steepling his fingers.

"We wondered if you were that other fellow," I went on.

He shook his head. "I've not experienced anything like that."

"Never?" Samuel asked.

"No."

He muttered something under his breath. "I had hoped you would have some answers."

"I'm afraid not. It's an intriguing development, though. I wonder what it means."

"Perhaps it doesn't mean anything," Samuel ground out. "Perhaps it was mere happenstance, but I want to stop it. It's damned inconvenient, particularly now that it has happened without us even being near one another."

"How diverting," Mrs. Myer said, her mouth twisted in what I assumed to be amusement. "This is a development, isn't it, Everett?"

"Indeed." He rubbed his chin, thoughtful.

"Myer," Samuel began, "I don't suppose you'll allow Charity to see your study?"

Mrs. Myer smothered her brittle laugh. "They don't believe you, Everett. How disheartening that must be for you."

He ignored his wife. I was beginning to think that was the best way to cope with her snide remarks. "Come with me," he said, standing.

Samuel and I followed him up the stairs. Mercifully, his wife remained in the drawing room. The staircase swept up five floors, but we only climbed to the third. It was an excessively large house for just two people and their servants. What a marvelous space it would be to house a small orphanage; not that the residents of Mayfair would accept such an establishment in their fine midst.

I'd expected the level to be as plainly decorated as the lower parts of the house, but it wasn't. Where the drawing room wallpaper was a dull single color, the third floor was printed in opulent gold and blue. The theme extended to Myer's study, with the addition of little peacocks prancing across the walls. There was also an abundance of artifacts crammed onto the shelves and desk, including statuettes, vases, boxes, framed sketches, and no less than five lamps and several stuffed animals. There was little space left on the surface of the small, spindly-legged desk for Mr. Myer to work. Indeed, aside from a silver inkwell and a matching pen, there was no other evidence that he worked there at all.

"This isn't the room in my vision," I told Samuel.

He nodded. "Thank you, Myer. I'm sorry for the intrusion."

"Not at all. Come in. Edith won't bother us in here."

"No, thank you," Samuel said. "Though I have one more question before we go. Do you know of others who have the power of visions? Someone in the society perhaps?"

"Society?" I echoed.

"The Society for Supernatural Activity. They have an interest in paranormal matters."

"For study purposes only," Myer said. "August Langley has been a member. Indeed, a great many scientists are attracted to our little group. I've found they have an insatiable desire to learn the truth in all things. They wish to explain the inexplicable, you could say, even if the answers turn out to be not of this world."

"Myer is their leader," Samuel told me. "Langley was indeed a member, but he's not anymore. He didn't agree with some of their methods. Nor do I."

"Come now, Gladstone. Like you, we merely yearn to know the truth. If, on occasion, the rules must be bent then no harm done."

Samuel tensed. He bared his teeth. "No harm! Tell that to Hannah, or the families of the men who died at the hands of that demon."

"Now, now, Gladstone, let's not discuss such matters in front of a lady." Myer gave me a simpering smile and patted my arm. "We're frightening Miss Evans."

I knew about the demon and other events that had occurred at Frakingham, of course, but hearing Samuel accuse Myer and the society of causing such troubles made my scalp tingle. It was too close for comfort; Samuel was only one link away from him. Indeed, the two men shared an unnatural ability of their own. An ability I hadn't trusted before, and needed to be wary of once more.

"Samuel, may we go?" I said. "I need to return to the school."

"School?" Myer cocked his head to the side. "Ah, yes, I recall now. You're a teacher."

I nodded.

"At a St. Giles school for orphans, I believe."

"Clerkenwell," I corrected. "Mr. and Mrs. Beaufort are the patrons."

"Then you are indeed fortunate." He bowed and signaled for me to leave the room ahead of him.

***

We didn't see Mrs. Myer again before departing and I was glad of it. Singularly, the Myers made me uneasy. Together, they made my skin crawl. Samuel drove me back through the elegant districts of the West End to the rookeries until we reached Clerkenwell, one of the most desperate areas of the city. It wasn't an ideal location for the orphanage, set amid the narrow, dark alleys. The soot of London had long ago settled into the cracks of the crooked, crumbling buildings and could not be scrubbed out, even by the most determined housewife.

The school was the largest building in the street and the most solid, made of good brick. Our stoop was the cleanest too, thanks to a well-paid maid. Children dressed in little more than rags gathered near the front door, talking and playing. None wore shoes, having stored them away for when the weather was cooler. None belonged inside, either. They weren't orphans. They lived nearby, although most were worse off than the orphans within the school walls. Our children had good clothes and shoes, regular meals and did not have to scavenge and steal to supplement their parents' meager incomes. It was heartbreaking to see such poverty, and I handed out coins before sending the local children on their way.

"You cannot save them all," Samuel said as he watched them edge up to the horses. "But I commend you for trying."

His words brought a lump to my throat. I'd never told anyone about my deepest wish, to save every child from poverty. It was such a fruitless dream, and there was no point in telling anyone. Besides, Samuel already knew. Samuel knew everything about me, now.

My chest tightened, my breaths coming short and shallow. I needed to stop thinking of how much Samuel knew or I'd go mad.

"Sorry," he muttered, dragging a hand through his hair. He'd removed his hat in the coach and it still occupied the seat. "I've been trying not to do that."

The strain of restraint showed in his exhausted features and the stoop of his shoulders. My heart softened. "Will you come inside?"

He shook his head. "You don't want me there."

"I thought you were going to stop doing that."

The corner of his mouth kicked up in a crooked half-smile. "I wasn't using my knowledge of you, that time. It was more my knowledge of what I've observed."

"Observations can be misinterpreted. If I didn't want you to come inside, I wouldn't have asked you."

He stepped closer, his eyelids lowered. Awareness of him sizzled within me. "In that case, I would like to come inside." His honey-thick voice slid across my skin, warming me all over. It was delicious and wonderful. I could listen to that voice all day, whispering sweet things into my ear, caressing my skin.

I closed my eyes. "Go on," I murmured.

"Are you sure? Is there somewhere private? I'd like to be alone with you, Charity."

For some reason, his voice changed. It was as if I'd been released from his spell. My eyes snapped open. I glared at him, hands on my hips. "You were hypnotizing me!"

He took a step back. "I was not."

"Then how do you explain my reaction?"

"How do you think?"

"Good lord, Samuel, you must think me a fool." I tried to keep my voice low, but it was difficult. "I am not like all your

76

other women. I am not so easily coerced by your voice and charms."

"I. Did. Not. Hypnotize. You."

"Whatever you did, it wasn't natural." I'd felt not altogether *there* when he'd been talking, like I was out of my body, or perhaps out of my mind. It was disconcerting. I didn't like feeling that way. "Leave, now. There's nothing more to discuss, anyway."

Indeed we'd spoken about Myer and the visions in the coach. We'd drawn no conclusions and had more questions than answers.

"As you wish," he bit off. "Good day, Charity." He spun on his heel and snatched up his hat from the seat. He slammed the coach door shut, causing the horses to twitch and shift. The children scattered and the driver moved on with a rumbling of wheels. Samuel didn't look back at me.

Part of me wanted to shout at the driver to stop, but that would be foolish. Samuel was gone, and that was the way it had to be. If he was going to use his powers over me, or use his knowledge of my thoughts and memories to inveigle himself into my good graces, then we could not be friends. I would worry all the time, wondering if he was about to hypnotize me. If he wanted more.

Why, oh why, had he done that? Why couldn't he be happy to simply be my friend?

I dabbed at the tear hovering in the corner of my eye. I would not cry over this—over him.

I looked up at the bold lettering painted on the bricks above the door, spelling out the name of the school. It was somewhat comforting. This was my home and it was a good one. It was my sanctuary.

A thick fog descended over my eyes. Another vision! I fought through it and came out the other side in an enclosed, dimly lit space. A fist slammed into a leather seat opposite me and pulled back. I recognized the seat and the hand. It belonged to Samuel and he was inside the Langley coach.

The fog descended and cleared again. I was looking up at the lettering above the school's door once more. I went inside and tried not to think about what I'd seen, but it was impossible. Samuel had been so upset that he'd grown violent. I'd not thought him like that, not thought him capable of physical harm. But I'd never seen him angry before, either. A shiver washed over me and a lump of unease settled in my stomach.

It was late and the children had already eaten supper. I helped them clean up and prepare for bed, determined to stay busy and not think about Samuel. He was a grown man and not my responsibility. If I kept telling myself that, I might believe it by the morning.

I climbed into bed, still a little shaken. I wished Jack wasn't so far away; he could have advised me or talked to Samuel on my behalf. He would know if Samuel had spoken the truth about not hypnotizing me, or if he'd lied in order to...

I pulled the covers up to my chin. It didn't bear thinking about.

I must have finally fallen asleep, because a sound awoke me some time later. The darkness in my room was so dense I could barely make out the shapes of the furniture.

Something was wrong. Apprehension slithered across my skin, but I couldn't fathom what had set my nerves on edge.

Then, suddenly, a shadow emerged from deeper within the shadows. A person. Close.

I opened my mouth to scream, but a shadowy hand clamped over it. Another dug into my hair and pulled. My scalp exploded in pain. I scrabbled at the hands, trying to peel them off, but he held me too tight. He was strong, big, his hands like bear paws. He dragged me from the bed and I stumbled to my knees on the floor. The carpet softened my fall, but it did nothing to stop the searing pain ripping across my scalp as my attacker pulled me up again by my hair. I screamed into his glove. His hand pressed harder against my mouth and now covered my nose, too. I couldn't breathe.

Somewhere, somehow, I summoned enough sense to realize that it was a bad time to struggle and use up the last of the air in my body, so I quieted.

He marched me over to the window and kicked aside the heavy curtain. Wan moonlight filtered through, caressing my face.

"You!" he growled.

He knew me? I tried to turn to see his face, but his grip was too tight on my hair. The hand over my mouth hadn't moved and my lungs screamed for air.

"What are you doing, Witch?" he snarled.

He let the curtain drop and dragged me towards the door. My feet grappled for purchase. My chest felt like it would explode. I tried again to remove the hand over my nose and mouth, but it was no good.

Air. I needed air.

"You're coming with me," he snarled. "Back where you belong."

Oh God. No. Who was he? Why was he kidnapping me?

I had the horrible, sickening sensation that I would know the answers to my questions if I hadn't asked Samuel to block my memories.

CHAPTER 6

My attacker's hand cut off my air. Dread filled my chest where my breath should. I had to get away. I struggled, but he was too strong. I clawed at his hand, scratching and tearing. With a hiss of pain, he mercifully moved it enough so that I could breathe through my nose. Perhaps he didn't want me dead after all.

So what *did* he want from me?

The vision of the girl in the bed came to mind and my stomach lurched. Fear settled in my heart like a brick. She was his prisoner.

Had I been too, once? Was this the man whose eyes I'd seen through?

I shoved the questions away. If I reached for the answers now, the fear would overwhelm me. I needed to keep my wits about me and act.

I kicked back hard and connected with his shin. He swore and repaid me by jerking me back by my hair again. I screamed, but the sound didn't travel far, with his hand covering my mouth.

He dragged me back toward the closed door; he would have to let go of my hair or my mouth to open it. It was my only chance.

I was wrong. He did let go of my hair, but not to open the door. He swung me around to face him and I got my first proper glimpse of my assailant. He was older than me by perhaps twenty years. I was tall for a woman, but he was taller, his massive frame towering over me. He had a face like a bulldog's, his features almost disappearing beneath the bulges of muscle and fat. His collar butted against the underside of his chin, with no neck to speak of. If I knew him—as I must if he knew me—then the memory block had worked exceedingly well. I didn't recognize him.

He'd let me go entirely. My mouth was free. I couldn't scream, though. I had not yet gasped in enough air for that. I backed up against the wall, but he lunged at me.

I kicked out, connecting with his nether region. He clutched himself in pain and hissed. I went to kick him again, but he caught my foot.

His fleshy lips curled into a sneer. "You always did make a sport of it. That's why the master liked you so much."

His words punched me in the gut. I felt ill. "Who are you? What do you want with me?"

"I'm returning you to where you belong. Piece of luck you bein' in the first room I checked here. Piece of luck finding you here at all. So you been dabblin' in witchcraft, eh? Been seein' through the master's eyes?"

I didn't get a chance to answer, or ask him more questions. He twisted my foot, unbalancing me. I fell to the floor, but grabbed for something on my way down. Anything. My fingers connected with the small table I used to display my few possessions. They tumbled off, clattering onto the floorboards. It probably hadn't made enough noise to wake the other teachers in the nearby rooms, so I opened my mouth to scream.

Stinging fire tore across my cheek as he slapped me. Dizziness clouded my head. I wanted to close my eyes, wanted to curl into a ball and sleep.

I had to get up. Had to fight or run. If he managed to get me out of the school, I would assuredly end up like that girl—a prisoner of his master.

He picked me up and tossed me over his shoulder. I went limp and let my arms and legs dangle loosely. I still felt a little dizzy from when he'd hit me, and being upside down didn't help clear my head. Nor did his smell, and I wrinkled my nose as the acrid stench of sweat filled my nostrils. But I didn't move a muscle, hoping he might think me unconscious.

He carried me into the dark corridor, where the moonlight did not reach the narrow passage. The other doors along it were closed, all behind them silent. I had mere moments before all would be lost.

"Help!" I screamed. "Get the pistol!" I fought him, but he held me clamped against his shoulder like a sack of straw. I beat his back with my fists, and prayed that more than one teacher would come to my aid. I doubted my attacker would be too troubled by a single female, even an armed one. But the call for the pistol had been a ruse; we had no weapons of that kind. I'd hoped to frighten him, but the big brute didn't falter. He ran with me towards the stairs.

Doors opened along the corridor. The other teachers gasped in horror, screamed and pleaded with the man to let me go. They did all the things I expected frightened women to do. Only one came to my aid: Mrs. Peeble.

Her room was the closest to the stairs. She opened it just as we passed and a gunshot rang out. Next thing I knew, my assailant cried out and dropped me. Sharp pain surged along my right side as I landed with a thud on the floor. I rolled out of the way and kicked out hard, connecting with the brute's knee. He swore and went to kick me back, but stopped.

Mrs. Peeble and five other teachers all approached slowly, weapons poised to strike. Mrs. Peeble was the only one with a pistol, while the others held vases or fire irons. She must have wounded him, forcing him to drop me.

The man's eyes widened. He glanced at me, then back at the women approaching him in their nightgowns, looking like specters from a Gothic novel.

My anger rose now that the immediate danger was over. How dare someone come into my sanctuary and try to kidnap me! "What do you want wiv me?" I heard my accent change from the carefully crafted one I used nowadays back to the cant of my youth.

He heard it too. He sneered. "You've not come so far from the gutter after all, eh?"

"The gun, Mrs. Peeble." I beckoned her to hand it to me. "I want to shoot this turd and watch 'im bleed."

Mrs. Peeble didn't flinch, bless her. She went to give me the small pistol.

The man turned and fled down the stairs. We all raced after him and chased him until he exited through the back door. He disappeared down the alley, knocking over crates in the darkness. No one followed. That would have been foolishness indeed.

"Are you all right, Miss Charity?" Mrs. Peeble asked.

One of the teachers circled her arm around me. I nodded. "I'll be all right after a cup of tea."

"Forget the tea. You need something more fortifying."

"We don't have anything more fortifying here."

"I do. Upstairs." She locked the back door. We did the rounds of the rest of the school, checking on the children. All slept soundly, thank God.

The headmaster and two male teachers emerged from the men's dormitory. They insisted on checking the surrounds again and making sure I was unharmed. Then came the questions. I expected them, but had no answers. They weren't aware that I'd had a memory block placed upon me. I'd asked for some leave to visit friends in the country and had not told them the real purpose for my absence. The supernatural frightened many good, God-fearing folk, and I didn't want to upset them. Only Mr. and Mrs. Beaufort, my employers, knew of my background before coming to the school. As far as the other teachers knew, I was a normal, virginal young woman like the other unwed staff.

I never did get my fortifying drink. Dawn came and I dressed while a policeman was fetched. Inspector Hart and his constable arrived shortly afterwards. I was able to give them a description, but few other answers. They must think me a liar for not knowing why I'd been chosen as the man's victim. In a way, I did lie. I omitted to tell them that part of my memory had been wiped.

"He said my room was the first one he looked into," I told them. "It was my bad luck, I suppose."

"And you fought him off?" Inspector Hart asked, stroking his thick moustache as if it were a pet.

"With much help from my fellow teachers." I smiled at Mrs. Peeble, who'd taken it upon herself to remain with me throughout the questioning. I'd never really liked the stern, humorless woman, with her strict adherence to the rules, but the night's events had me changing my mind. I owed her a great deal, and it would seem she was prepared to bend the rules from time to time. She owed me a fortifying drink, for one thing. "Mrs. Peeble keeps a pistol in her room. She shot him."

"I did," she said, lifting her square chin. Her small, black eyes shone like polished jet. I had a suspicion she had rather enjoyed herself. "I sleep with the derringer under my pillow, just in case. A woman alone can never be too careful. You ought to remember that, Miss Charity."

"I think I'll take your advice on such matters henceforth, Mrs. Peeble."

"I shot him in the arm," she told the inspector. She indicated the position on her own arm. "Then Miss Charity kicked him in the knee."

The inspector's brows rose. "Remind me never to cross you two in a dark corridor at night." He and the constable chuckled.

Mrs. Peeble and I glared at them. Considering the circumstances, it was a tasteless joke. Their chuckles died.

"Yes, well, we'll do our best to find him, Miss Evans, but you've not given us much to go on."

"I wish I had more," I said. The truth of that struck me in the chest. I *did* wish I could give him a name to go with the face. Yet that would mean having all my memories, and I didn't want those back. Not even now.

Unless...

Samuel. Samuel knew all the pieces. He could give the police a name to go with the face. Not only would it resolve the problem, but it also meant I didn't have to know *why* the man had tried to kidnap me.

"I have a friend who will want to speak to you about this matter," I said. "He might be able to tell you who to question."

The inspector frowned. "Forgive me for asking, Miss Evans, but... was he here?"

Mrs. Peeble gasped. "How dare you imply something of that nature! It's uncalled for."

The poor inspector couldn't get his apology out quickly enough. He looked a little intimidated by Mrs. Peeble. I didn't blame him.

"My friend is a, er, psychic," I said. "He may have seen something, if you know what I mean."

"No, Miss Evans, I do not." Hart exchanged a curious glance with Mrs. Peeble, who flared her nostrils at him. "But I will listen to what he has to say."

"I'll go to him directly," I said. "If he can help, I'll send him to your station."

"Right you are, miss, but I must make a suggestion, if you don't mind. If this fellow can't help, you need to get away from here. Even if he can, you should still leave. Just until we can arrest the intruder. It's not safe for you here, now."

I stared down at my hands folded on my lap. The knuckles were white. "I suppose not," I whispered. "But I have nowhere to go."

"Perhaps you can visit those friends of yours in the country again," Mrs. Peeble said, with surprising gentleness.

Go to Frakingham House? Would they have me? I gave a small nod. I had no other options. I would not go to the Beauforts and endanger their young children; no matter how friendly they were, I couldn't ask that of them. Tommy and Jack were my only true friends. Even with Jack gone, I felt sure that I would be accepted into his home.

"That's settled then," the inspector said, standing. "Leave today, Miss Evans. Not only are you in danger if you remain here, but so are the rest of the residents."

Oh God. The children. Mrs. Peeble reached out and took my hand in her own. "It's for the best," she said. "For everyone."

She was right. I had to leave my home and my children. But first, I needed to speak to Samuel and learn the name of my attacker.

***

I alighted from the hansom cab in front of Claridge's Hotel, where Samuel was staying. A footman took my valise while another directed me inside. I inquired after Samuel, and pretended not to notice the way the butler's mouth turned down in disgust. It was not proper for an unwed woman to ask after a gentleman at a hotel. He must think me the sort of woman I *used* to be.

"Mr. Gladstone has gone out," he said, peering down his nose at me. "Would you care to wait?"

I was about to answer when a well-dressed woman of middling age came up beside me and jerked me around roughly by the arm. "Were you enquiring after *Samuel* Gladstone?" she asked.

I bristled at her direct tone. It was the tone of someone used to having every question answered, every whim catered to. She wore an exquisite gray and peach dress, made of silk, with white lace cuffs and a row of silver buttons down the front. She had a hawkish nose beneath quick gray eyes that took in my dress, valise and face. She did not smile.

"Well?" she prompted. "Were you inquiring after Samuel Gladstone?"

"Calm yourself, my dear," said a man standing behind her. He was a tall, striking gentleman with thick gray hair and side whiskers, and a stern countenance. His face was handsome for a man who appeared to be in his forties, but it was his eyes that had me take a step back. They were the brightest blue, the same color as Samuel's before he'd hypnotized me.

"Are you Mr. and Mrs. Gladstone?" I asked. "Samuel's parents?"

"Did I not ask *you* a question?" the woman said. "Am I invisible to you?"

"My dear," the gentleman scolded. "Do not upset yourself."

The woman seemed to collect her wits at the sound of his voice. She smoothed her skirt and looked around. None of the staff or hovering guests appeared to be listening, but I was quite sure they were all straining as much as they could to hear our conversation.

"I know Mr. Gladstone through Jack Langley," I said. I received blank stares in return. "Samuel's friend, Jack Langley. From Frakingham House. We've known one another for years, but I only met Samuel a few months ago."

Finally, a spark of recognition. Mrs. Gladstone, if that's indeed who she was, blinked slowly. She put out her hand, as if to grip hold of something for balance. Her husband took it. "Freak House," she whispered. "I've heard of it. Why would he be there?"

I tried not to show my surprise, but I'm sure I must have. How had they not known their son was at Frakingham?

The gentleman turned to the butler. "Is there a Samuel Gladstone staying here too?"

"Yes, Mr. Gladstone."

Mrs. Gladstone pressed a hand to her heart. "He's here," she whispered. To the butler, she said, "Why did nobody tell us?"

"I, er, that is it's not our way, Mrs. Gladstone."

She enclosed her hand around her husband's arm and peered up at him through swimming eyes. "He's here, Henry."

I thought I saw the man's mouth twitch, but he merely nodded. "And this young lady is going to tell us why."

I gulped. "I'm not sure that I can do that."

"You seem to have some notion of what he's been doing, at least," Mrs. Gladstone said.

"Is there a private parlor where we can wait?" Mr. Gladstone asked the butler.

"Of course." The butler clicked his fingers to get the attention of a hovering footman. "Privett will show you the way." He turned a false smile onto me. "Will madam be requiring a room?"

"No, thank you," I said. At Mrs. Gladstone's little whimper of shock, I quickly added, "I'm catching a train out of London today. Please store my valise, for the time being." I did not want anyone thinking that Samuel and I were lovers, least of all his parents.

We followed Privett into a small adjoining room, set out with four comfortable looking armchairs. A harpsichord snuggled into a corner beside an unlit fireplace and a low bookshelf provided reading matter for waiting guests. I sat in one chair and Mrs. Gladstone sat in another. The derringer pistol given to me by Mrs. Peeble pressed against my thigh. I'd tucked it into the pocket sewn into my dress, as she'd instructed.

Mr. Gladstone remained standing, his hands behind his back. His expression was guarded as he studied me with those unnerving blue eyes.

His wife studied me again too, but she was much easier to read. I knew she didn't like me, I could see it in her tight lips and rigid jaw. She removed her gloves and set them on her lap. I kept mine on. It seemed best to hide my scars from prying eyes for the moment.

"Who are you?" she asked.

"My name is Charity Evans."

She dismissed my answer with a flick of her long, fine fingers. "I mean, who are your family?"

I thought about lying. I could have made up a story about the Evanses of Derbyshire, with their rich lands and a heritage that could be traced back through the centuries. It was what I used to do as a child, after my mother abandoned me. She'd been a charwoman when she could find work. When she couldn't, she was just a drunk. I'd never known my father. He could have been a duke or a beggar. The only time my mother did mention him, she'd followed it up by spitting in the dirt.

"I have no family," I said.

Mrs. Gladstone snorted. "Everyone has a family."

"Not me." They would draw no further comment from me on my background. It was none of their affair.

Mr. Gladstone must have sensed my reluctance. "My dear," he said to his wife. "It's not important."

"Not important!" Her loud outburst must have shocked even her. She quickly glanced at the door then took a deep breath and splayed her fingers across her lap. "Very well. Let me ask another question. How do you know our son?"

"I told you. Through our mutual friend, Jack Langley of Frakingham House."

"And I told you. We know no Langleys, although we have heard of the estate."

"Did they buy it from Lord Frakingham?" Mr. Gladstone asked.

"I believe so," I said. "Jack's uncle is a successful microbiologist. He owns the estate and Jack manages it for him. Samuel has lived with them since before Christmas, I believe."

The two exchanged glances. Mr. Gladstone's lips flattened, but his wife seemed to grow more agitated.

She turned back to me and inched forward in the chair. "But... *why* is he there? *Why* did he leave the employ of Dr. Werner? And his studies, too?"

"I don't know."

She slammed her hand down on the arm of the chair. "You *must* know!"

"I assure you, I do not." I would not be brow beaten. I owed her no answers.

Mr. Gladstone pressed his wife's shoulder. "There there, my dear." He watched me over the top of her head, but I still could not fathom his thoughts.

No matter. I didn't particularly care whether they believed me or not; their estrangement from their son was none of my affair.

Yet I could not stop wondering if it had something to do with Samuel's hypnotic abilities.

"Bloody hell," came a gravelly voice from the doorway. "Am I living a nightmare?"

We three turned, as one, to see Samuel standing there, glaring at us through bloodshot eyes. He scrubbed both hands down his face and by the time he'd dropped them, his mother stood before him. For one heart-stopping moment, I didn't know if she was going to slap him or embrace him. It would seem Samuel was equally uncertain. He leaned backward a little and eyed her warily.

She embraced him. "My boy! We found you!" She gave a little sob into his shoulder.

Samuel patted her back gingerly and looked to me. "Sorry," he said. It wasn't clear if he was speaking to me or his mother. "Is everything all right, Charity? I wasn't expecting to see you so soon after our... parting."

"Actually—"

"Now is not a good time," Mr. Gladstone snapped.

"Something's wrong," Samuel said through a tight jaw. He tried to extricate himself from his mother, but she refused to let him go. "Can we do this later? I need to speak with Charity."

She pulled back to get a better look at him. I couldn't see her face, but I suspected she was as horrified as I felt. How could he speak to his mother like that? His father looked as if he'd explode.

"We haven't seen you in an age!" Mrs. Gladstone cried.

He sighed. "How are you both? And is Bert well?" This last question was asked with more earnestness than the first.

"Well enough. He has missed his brother," Mrs Gladstone said. "Oh, Samuel, why didn't you tell us where you were? It's been months. It's not like you."

He grunted. "It's exactly like me, Mother. Don't pretend otherwise. Charity—"

"Samuel!" Mr. Gladstone ground out. "Your mother has asked you a very reasonable question. Answer her."

Samuel's body went rigid. His dark eyes flashed. "I've been at Frakingham House. I found Mr. Langley and his family to be very accepting of my kind."

"Your... kind?" Mr. Gladstone's gaze slid to me.

"You can talk freely around Charity. She knows what I am. She accepts it. Accepts me."

I thought him overstating my tolerance of his hypnosis, but I didn't say so. I would not get involved in their family squabbles. Indeed, I rather thought I should leave. But it was so terribly interesting. My curiosity had been prodded until it was standing to attention. I wanted to learn all I could about Samuel, and this seemed to be a good way to do it.

"Please excuse us, Miss Evans," Mr. Gladstone said to me with barely strained patience. "As you can see, we have family affairs to discuss with our son."

It would seem I had to listen at the door instead. I rose to leave, but Samuel shook his head.

"She stays," he said. "She's my... friend."

Why did he hesitate? Was I not his friend? Or did he consider me to be something more? His parents must have taken it as the latter, and their wrinkled noses were a clear indication of what they thought of it, too.

I glared at Samuel. He merely shrugged and gave me an innocent look in apology.

"Are you mad?" his father snarled.

"Quite possibly." Samuel grinned. It was indeed the grin of a madman. "But the fact remains, Charity is not someone you can order about. She stays."

"Actually, I think it's best if I do leave." I shrugged an apology back at him and mimicked his puppy-dog look. "Clearly you need to spend some time alone with your parents."

"The last time I spent a few minutes alone with them, they accused me of all manner of ills. They then had me thrown in prison."

I gawped at him. "Prison?"

"Newgate, to be precise."

"Only for a few days," his mother said with a wave of her hand.

"You thoroughly deserved it," his father added.

Samuel sighed. "Something you reminded me of frequently, after my release. So, you see, forgive me if I don't wish to endure that again. It grew tiring."

"There!" His father pointed a finger at him. "That is precisely why you ought to be reminded of what you did. You're much too glib about it. I see not a whit of remorse in you."

Samuel bowed his head, hiding his reaction. What had he done? It must have been heinous indeed. But if it had been, wouldn't he have remained in prison for longer than a few days? It didn't make sense.

"You don't know what is in my head or my heart," Samuel said quietly. Ominously. "Do not pretend otherwise. Do not pretend that you want me home again, because you, sir, do not. You were relieved when I went to University College. Finally I was out of your house."

"We were relieved because it meant you were making something of yourself. Why did you leave?"

"I was learning nothing there. I already knew more about how the mind worked than my lecturers. My hypnosis—"

"Don't! Don't mention that word. It's an abomination."

I tried to catch Samuel's gaze, but he wasn't looking at me. My heart weighed heavily in my chest. How could people who professed to love him be so cruel to their son? I may not have parents, but I expected a mother and father would love their child, no matter what. And Samuel certainly deserved their love. Whatever he was, he was a good man. He was not the disgusting creature his father made him out to be.

"What your... *power* has led you to do is an abomination," his father went on. "It's time you buried that part of you for good. Look at you. Look at what it's doing to you. You could be mistaken for a vagrant."

Samuel barked a harsh laugh. "There's no need to insult the vagrants."

Mr. Gladstone clicked his tongue and was about to speak again, but his wife put her hand on his arm to stop him.

"Please, come home with us," she pleaded. "You'll be safe there, around people who can help you."

"Help me?" Samuel scoffed. "You misunderstand, Mother, yet again. I do not *need* help. I am what I am. Nothing will change that."

"Don't be absurd," his father spat. "You're a Gladstone. Gladstones are solid people. They're not... hypnotists." He whispered the word, as if speaking it aloud would leave a bad taste in his mouth.

"This one is. I will not be returning home with you. I live at Frakingham House, now. I'll be leaving for Hertfordshire today."

His mother emitted a small sob. "Why there and not with us? We're your family."

"By blood only."

She stepped back as if he'd struck her. Her husband put a hand on her shoulder to steady her. I watched them, wishing I had the courage to defend Samuel, but I did not. I wasn't so sure they were wrong. Samuel did indeed look harried, and I wasn't comfortable with his ability to hypnotize, any more than they. I could see why they would want him to be rid of such a dubious skill.

There was no point in giving my opinion, however. They were the sort of people who wouldn't listen to a lowly teacher.

I watched the stand-off between parents and son until the gazes of Mr. and Mrs. Gladstone shifted to the doorway. I turned to look, as did Samuel.

A beautiful, dark-haired woman stood there. She was perhaps the most elegant lady I'd ever seen. She was as tall as me, with a tiny waist and deep bosom, shown off to perfection by the sea-green dress. The color matched the pert little hat atop her head and her lovely eyes. She pressed a hand to her lips and gasped, but even that movement was graceful.

"You're here," she whispered. "My darling, you've come back."

"Ebony," Samuel said, darkly. "Why are you here?"

"To see us," Mr. Gladstone told him. "We come to London, from time to time, and like to see your fiancée while we're here."

CHAPTER 7

Samuel was engaged.

It took several moments for me to digest the news and another several to tear my gaze away from the beautiful woman who couldn't stop smiling at Samuel. She looked as if she'd opened a chest and found treasure inside.

I felt a little sorry for her. Samuel may have been engaged to her, but he'd flirted with me, and probably other women, too. He was hardly devoted.

"Don't call her my fiancée," Samuel said over his shoulder to his parents. "Ebony was your choice, not mine."

I cringed at his harsh words as Ebony's eyes filled with tears. She stepped closer to him, but he stepped back. "I was your choice, once," she said, her voice throaty. "And you were mine. You still are."

He turned his face away from her and I caught a glimpse of his eyes as he glanced at me. They were full of shadows and emotions that I couldn't begin to fathom.

Ebony followed his gaze and her nostrils flared. She gave me a brief nod of greeting and appeared to be waiting for an introduction. Samuel didn't make one.

"Excuse me," I whispered, slipping past them. It was growing too crowded in that small room; I felt like I was suffocating.

"Charity!" he called after me. "Don't leave, yet."

I lifted my chin. "I'll wait for you outside." I hazarded another glance at Ebony. She watched me with a sad twist to her mouth. It would seem she was as disturbed by my presence as I was by hers.

My reaction unnerved me. I shouldn't be shocked. I'd always known Samuel's family was well-to-do. The son of an important family always married, and married well. It was their duty.

I waited in the hotel foyer until Samuel emerged a few minutes later, alone.

"Come with me." He grabbed my arm hard at the elbow and pulled me towards the door. "We'll go for a walk."

I jerked free. "Do not force me," I hissed.

He stopped and stared at me, his eyes round. "I… I'm sorry. I didn't realize what I was doing. Please accept my deepest apology."

I winced. Perhaps I'd spoken too harshly. I knew he hadn't meant to hurt me and that was the important thing. Clearly he was troubled by the meeting in the parlor.

"Bloody hell," he murmured, pinching the bridge of his nose. "I'm so sorry, Charity. I don't know what's wrong with me."

"I accept your apology. A walk is a nice suggestion."

I glanced back into the hotel before the door closed and caught sight of Samuel's parents and fiancée staring at us. Mr. Gladstone scowled, but the two women seemed rather forlorn. I felt sorry them—both of them. And yet, Samuel must have a good reason for snubbing them.

It must have something to do with them sending him to prison. I was considering how to ask him about it when another thought struck me.

"We touched and didn't get a vision. Do you think that's the end of them? Are we cured?"

"Perhaps," he said. "Or perhaps they come at random moments now, like the last one."

A chilling thought. "Why now, when we had to touch before?"

"The connection is stronger, perhaps? Or the third time was the charm, as the saying goes. We'd touched three times, had three visions, and then the fourth was triggered by something else."

"What?"

"I don't know."

That was as disturbing as having the visions themselves.

Brook Street was busy with Mayfair madams and their friends, taking leisurely strolls in the feeble spring sunshine. The gentlemen were more likely to be at their clubs or work, if they did indeed work at all. Coaches and horses sped along the road, sometimes at alarming rates, their wheels flicking up dirt and muck. It wasn't the most pleasant walk, but there was nowhere else for a gentleman and an unwed woman to go without raising eyebrows.

"Something's happened," Samuel said, before I could ask any questions of my own about his parents and the woman named Ebony. "What's wrong?"

"I need you to take me to Frakingham. When do you leave?"

He held up his hands for me to slow down. "Of course I'll take you, you'll be very welcome there. But I thought you were determined not to see the place again. Or me," he added quietly.

I swallowed. "I... I'm sorry that we didn't part on friendly terms. It's ironic that I'm now in need of your help and must humbly apologize to you."

"Don't apologize, there's no need. It's my fault. I was much too forward, yesterday."

True, but I wasn't going to admit that. I needed to remain in his good graces for the time being. "Thank you," I said. "You see, the police have suggested I leave London until they can ensure my safety."

"The police? Your safety? Hell." He went to reach for my hand, but he drew back before touching. "You'd better start at the beginning."

I told him about the intruder, and watched anxiously as the color drained from his face. By the end of my tale, his lips were bloodless. His hands shook. He closed them into fists. "Dear God, Charity. Did he… did he hurt you?"

"No." It seemed unnecessary to tell him that my scalp had burned for hours afterwards, or that I had a bruise on my hip from where he'd dropped me on the floor.

"Everybody is well. I'm well. But he escaped and he may try again. That's why I need to leave."

He nodded somewhat numbly. "We'll leave today. Immediately."

"I was hoping you would say that."

He closed his eyes. "Have the police any clue as to who he might be?"

I didn't answer straight away and he opened his eyes. It was obvious that his question was for my benefit. He already knew who the man was, or at least, knew that he was connected to my lost memories.

"None," I said.

I watched and waited for his next question. He started moving again, his pace quickening, and I had to trot to keep up. I touched his wrist, indicating for him to slow down.

"Samuel," I said heavily. "I have to describe him to you."

"Why?"

"You know why."

He looked straight ahead. "No."

"The man knew me and spoke as if I knew him. He's from my past. He's the one I asked you to block from my memories."

He shook his head. "It's not possible."

"Why not?"

Another shake of his head. "What makes you think this man is linked?"

"I just do. I can't explain why."

"The memories could be of a woman, or your family, not a man."

"I just know it is." I didn't tell him that I'd guessed, based on my reluctance to be intimate with men, and that echoes of fear rippled through me whenever a man restrained me, even when that restraint was as harmless as Samuel steering me out the door. "I also know that he hurt me."

He glanced at my gloved hands.

"There are scars on my back too."

He didn't say anything for several heartbeats. When he did, it was after a long sigh. "I wondered if you would notice them."

"Not at first. Samuel, you need to tell the police about the man who… gave me those scars. You need to give them a name. I want him arrested for attempting to abduct me last night. I cannot live with the knowledge that he could return any moment. The children…" I finished on a choke.

"Bloody hell," he muttered. "It can't be him. It just can't."

"Why not?"

He rubbed his temples with both hands, as if scrubbing away a memory. My memory. "If there is a connection… how did he find you?"

"I don't know. That's not important. What is important is a name."

He swore softly. "I can't give you one. He never used a name. It's not him, anyway."

I sucked air between my teeth. "The attacker mentioned he was returning me to his master."

Samuel stopped. Stared. His Adam's apple jerked up and down.

"He was a big fellow," I forged on. "He had a brutish face and small piggy eyes."

A muscle in his jaw jumped. "Dark hair? Massive hands?"

I nodded. "So you do know him?"

"Him, yes. But I can't tell the police how to find him."

"What about the master he was referring to?" I swallowed heavily. "Surely you can give them an address or name for him."

He shook his head. "I told you, it can't be him."

"And I'm telling you it is. I feel so sure. Your reaction just now would imply that you know someone known as the master."

He said nothing. His gaze slid to the footpath and he closed his hands into fists so tight the knuckles turned stark white.

"Do you know how to get to the man's house or place of work?" I went on.

Another shake of his head. I had the suspicion he wanted to explain why, but did not want to divulge even the smallest piece of information from my lost memory.

"What sort of man was he? A sewer rat or a toff?"

"Don't ask me, Charity. No more questions. I can't answer them and there's no point. Someone is playing a trick. I recognize the attacker, but his master... it's not the same man who gave you those scars. It can't be."

"Why not?"

"Because he's dead."

***

No matter how many questions I asked, Samuel wouldn't answer them. All he would tell me was that the man known as 'the master' was dead. He wouldn't even tell me how it had happened.

We traveled out of London in August Langley's coach. My heart weighed heavily in my chest as the gray pall shrouding the city disappeared over the horizon. I would miss the children terribly, but I prayed that my absence would mean no more visits to the school from that brute.

We spent much of the first leg of our journey in silence. Samuel was a far cry from the amiable gentleman of our first meeting, months prior. There were none of his charms on display, no friendly banter, just an uncomfortable silence in which I pretended to sleep or he did.

But there was only so long one could ignore one's traveling companion. There was also only so long before my curiosity became too much.

"Congratulations," I said.

He had been staring at the scenery whipping past the window, but now turned to face me. "On what?"

"Your engagement. When were you going to announce it?"

"I'm not engaged."

"The lady and your parents seem to think otherwise."

"I do have *some* say in whom I marry."

I arched an eyebrow.

He sighed. "If I don't mind being cut off, that is."

Ah, now we got to the crux of it. "Your father would cut your allowance if you didn't marry Ebony?"

"Cut it and exclude me from the will. I was to be given one of the lesser houses upon Father's death, while my brother inherited the main estate, but he's made it known that my brother will get everything if I don't marry Ebony."

"Is her family that important?"

"Her father is a viscount."

"Ah. Say no more. Surely you could see your way to accommodating your parents' wishes in the matter? After all, the daughter of a viscount would be a great prize." I was only being partly sarcastic. A wealthy family could do almost anything, but a noble one could reach to even greater heights. Samuel's life would be far superior to anything I could even imagine if he wed her. I couldn't quite see why he had such a problem with it.

"She is not a game to be won or lost," he said. "There are no prizes."

"Perhaps not a game, no." But marriage was a form of gambling. If one married up, for example, and was able to pull oneself out of poverty through a well-chosen marriage, then who could deny that it was a win? If I wanted to take the path of marriage to better myself, then I would choose someone living in a nice house with a secure position, perhaps a bank clerk or teacher. That was as high as someone like me could climb.

But I didn't want that. I didn't want to give up the school or my savings. I didn't want to stop working so that I could keep house. I didn't want to be a man's wife, or a man's anything. I wanted to be *me*. I'd gone through a lot to get where I was and have a measure of freedom. I would not give it up. I had children—the orphans—and I had my own room. With regard to love between a man and woman, I wanted to believe in it, but I was yet to feel that emotion. It was quite possible I wasn't capable, even now without the dark memory holding me back.

"It doesn't always pay to be stubborn, Samuel."

He arched a brow. "You think I'm being stubborn?"

"She is a beauty."

"There is more to a successful marriage than a beautiful wife."

"Not all men would agree with you on that score."

His mouth curved up at the corner. "I am not like other men."

And I knew it. "I really don't see what's wrong with her."

"You don't know her."

I waited but he didn't elaborate. "Well? What is wrong with her?"

"I'm not at liberty to divulge that."

I gave him a tight smile. "How gentlemanly of you." And frustrating. The curiosity was going to gnaw at me. "Does your father know?"

"You would have to ask him."

Neither yes nor no. Hmmm. He may be guarded, but he also seemed a little amused by our exchange. His eyes were brighter than they had been since I'd told him about my attack. "So he's willing to cut you off because you won't wed his choice of girl. It seems a little excessive."

He leaned his elbow on the window frame and buried his hand in his hair, messing it up. "My father likes to control things. Control me."

"And you are not controllable?"

That quirk of his mouth again. "I'm a hypnotist. I've been able to control others from a young age. It has never been the other way around."

I swallowed. Putting it so bluntly made me realize how powerful he was. Samuel could do whatever he wanted. He could even get away with murder, or worse. "Did you hypnotize your parents?"

He turned to look out the window again. "What child wouldn't want to have that power over his parents? Particularly one as tyrannical as my father."

"But you could not hypnotize him all the time."

"No. And he would make me suffer for it, which is only right. I deserved my punishments."

I shivered and crossed my arms against the sudden chill.

"One of those punishments is to disinherit me if I don't follow his wishes. I did do as he asked, in most things. I went to University College. I took a position in Dr. Werner's medical practice. I agreed to marry Ebony."

"What happened? Why did it all change?"

He shook his head. "It's a long story, and not one I wish to dredge up. Suffice to say, it culminated in my leaving London and coming to Frakingham. Anything prior to that is history."

"History lessons are something neither of us like, I think."

He looked relieved that I understood. In a way, I did, but not entirely. He'd had a privileged upbringing, with a good education and wealth at his disposal. He had a family, and no matter how controlling his father was, Samuel was loved by his mother. The meeting at Claridge's had shown me that. Yet he'd discarded it all. He ought to live on the streets for a month, then he'd be reluctant to throw away the riches at his disposal.

"Why don't you just hypnotize your father and get him to sign part of your inheritance over to you now?"

He smirked. "Because that would be wrong and I'm not entirely without morals, no matter what you may think."

I smiled. It had been a test, and he'd passed. "Surely your mother would have something to say about your disinheritance. Sshe seemed very eager to have you return home. Surely if she knew you kept away because of your father's insistence you wed Ebony, she would be on your side. Couldn't she speak to him?"

"That's not the only reason I've kept away."

"Oh? What else then?"

"You're full of questions today. Usually you're not so interested in my affairs."

Wasn't I? I tried to think about all the times we'd spoken of personal matters, and had to admit that he was right. Not that I wasn't interested in him, but recent circumstances had not allowed conversations to bend in that direction. Besides, our first few meetings had been awkward beyond bearing. I had not wanted him near me at all. It was only now that my memory was blocked that I could concede that I liked him and wanted to know more about him.

Against my better judgment.

"Then perhaps it's best if we drop the subject altogether," I said. "History and all that."

He gave me a fleeting smile. "The here and now is more important. Keeping you safe."

"Thank you, Samuel. You've been very kind to me." On a whim, I reached across the gap between us and took his hand. I'd removed my gloves near the beginning of our journey as the cabin was warm. He stroked my knuckles with his thumb, sending little tingling sensations whispering across my skin. I smiled at him and he smiled back. His thumb stroked up to the back of my hand where the scar marred the skin.

I withdrew it and hurriedly picked up my gloves from the seat beside me. Samuel leaned forward and placed his hand over mine.

"You don't have to hide them from me, Charity. You don't need to hide anything."

I swallowed the lump in my throat. "Please don't remind me that you know everything about me."

"I don't," he rasped. "I know one particular period of your life and that's all. You're as much a mystery to me as any woman."

I didn't believe that, but I was grateful for his attempt to soothe my nerves.

"Thank you," I whispered. "You've been a good friend to me."

His face softened. His eyes smiled even though his mouth didn't move. "We *are* friends now, aren't we?"

"Yes."

"Good. I'm glad."

"But nothing more," I added.

He inclined his head in a nod. "I know. You've made that very clear."

I wanted to tell him that anything more than friendship between us was impossible, that I would never be his mistress and the gap between us didn't allow more. But our friendship was a mere sapling; I didn't want to subject it to strong winds yet.

"You stopped being self-conscious about those scars after I hypnotized you," he said with a nod at my hands. "What's changed now?"

I stared down at the ugly skin. I hadn't realized my anxiety over them had returned until he'd pointed it out. "I don't know."

Our gazes locked. I saw the concern in his eyes and felt the dread inside me. The memory block might still be in place, but the recent attack had stirred up feelings the block had suppressed. Feelings that were so deeply rooted within me that they'd become a part of me, despite my attempts to smother them.

***

I'd been apprehensive about Sylvia's reaction to my sudden reappearance at Frakingham with Samuel, but she welcomed me with a friendly smile. It didn't quite meet her eyes, but that was understandable. I hardly knew her and she me. We would have time to change that now. I was determined to like her. Hannah liked her, although she did say that Jack's cousin was silly at times.

"You can have the same room as your previous visit," she said as we entered the house. "Mrs. Moore will need some time to prepare it. Cook will also need to be told that we have an extra in our midst. Your arrival has thrown us into disarray, Charity, but no matter. The staff are highly capable." She softened the barb with another smile.

I wasn't sure how to take it, so I merely thanked her.

"Disarray?" Samuel scoffed. "One extra is hardly a great disturbance."

"It may not be where you used to live, Samuel, but it is here." Sylvia sniffed. "We have few servants for a house of this size."

"If it's a problem, hire more."

"We would, if we could."

Samuel frowned. "Why don't you?"

She said nothing. It was Tommy who answered. "Nobody from the village wants to work at Freak House."

"Tommy," Sylvia snapped. "Don't you have work to do?"

Tommy dutifully picked up my valise and headed for the stairs. "It's true," he shot back over his shoulder.

"That's no reason to announce it to all and sundry!"

He didn't answer, but made his way up the staircase. I wasn't sure what to say.

"I don't know why," Samuel said. "Jack would make a very reasonable employer."

Sylvia sighed and headed towards the corridor that led to the drawing room. "It's Uncle they're afraid of, and Bollard."

"I'm sure the vicious attacks at Christmas didn't help," he said.

She stumbled and Samuel caught her by the elbows to steady her. She jerked free and quickly glanced at me. "Did you have to bring that up when we have company?"

"I'm not really company," I said. "I'm..." What was I? Not a friend or relation. At best, I could be labeled an acquaintance. At worst, I was someone in need of charity.

"You're welcome here, that's what you are," Samuel said. "Treat Frakingham like your home."

Sylvia sat on the sofa in a puff of cream and blue skirts. She was such a pretty girl, of about eighteen, with her tight blonde curls and a sweet face. Her eyes were blue and round, innocent. Yet there was something in her countenance that troubled me. She didn't like me, and I had no idea why. The only reason I could see was that I was an orphan from the gutter who didn't belong in her drawing room any more than a stain on the upholstery.

I wouldn't let it upset me. I'd come across women like her before. It was a shame, because she was Jack's cousin, but so be it. There was nothing I could do to change her mind.

Tommy brought us tea and lingered in the drawing room after serving it. Sylvia didn't say anything, but she did glare at him until he bowed and apologized to her.

"I wanted to speak to Charity," he said. "We hardly got to talk last time and we've much to say to one another."

We did indeed. Some of my charges were orphans that he and Jack had initially taken into their care. After our little family split up, and Jack moved to Frakingham with Tommy, August Langley had continued to support those who remained behind. Some had since moved into my own school, but many of the older ones preferred the independence that living on the street gave them.

"I'll come and see you later," I told him.

"Right you are."

The hint of his street accent had me smiling, but Sylvia scowled, as did Samuel. I couldn't see why; I doubted the way he talked bothered Samuel.

Nevertheless, they were both silent as they drank their tea.

Thankfully August Langley arrived, his wheelchair pushed by Bollard. The mute positioned the chair by the fireplace, where a small fire kept the chill from the late afternoon air.

"It's a pleasure to see you again, Miss Evans," he said to me.

"And you too, sir. Please, call me Charity."

He tugged the edges of his red and gold smoking jacket over his middle, but they didn't meet. I'd never seen him smoke, so he must simply like the look of the garment. It certainly brightened the otherwise darkly furnished room. It surprised me to see him wearing it. It wasn't the sort of jacket that I expected a man with a dour, cool countenance would wear.

"What brings you to our residence again?" he asked. "Has Samuel's block not worked as well as you'd hoped?"

I exchanged glances with Samuel then drew a deep breath and told Langley about the intruder, including my suspicion that he was linked to the man in my blocked memory. When I finished, he simply rubbed his hand over his heavy chin in thought. It was the only sign that he was perturbed by what I'd said.

Sylvia, on the other hand, leapt off the sofa and knelt at my feet. "You poor thing! I do hope you are all right."

"Thank you," I said. "I'm unharmed."

"Thank goodness. Samuel, you did the right thing bringing her here. The disruption to our household harmony is inconsequential in the light of what Charity has been through."

I suppressed a giggle. She was fickle indeed, but it didn't seem like the right time to find amusement in her sudden change of heart.

"She came to me," he said. "I was preparing to leave London when she arrived at Claridge's. The timing was… fortunate."

Had he been about to say something else? Inconvenient, perhaps?

"You'll be safe here," Langley assured me. "This is the best place you can be, for now. Are the police following any particular lines of inquiry?"

"I don't know. I left before I could talk to Inspector Hart again. He did assure me that he would do what he could, but without a name, the chances of finding the man are slim."

Everyone looked at Samuel. Samuel held up his hands. "I can't help. I can give a description of the man known as the master, but no name."

"Then you must give the police that description!" Sylvia said.

"He's dead."

She gasped. Langley's head jerked up, and even Bollard's lips parted.

"I saw his body in Charity's memory. I know he's dead."

"Perhaps Charity was mistaken."

Samuel shook his head. "Even if she were, two people are less likely to be mistaken by what they saw. Jack also saw his dead body. Indeed, it was Jack's fire that killed him."

I tucked my hands away, hiding the scars. Had they been caused by that fire?

"Interesting," Langley said. "A curious matter. Tell me, what are your thoughts on the man you swap visions with? Could *he* be Charity's attacker?"

"It's a possibility." Samuel's gaze flicked to mine.

"I'm certain of it," I said. "The intruder mentioned the visions. Either he or his master connected the school to the visions and the brute went to investigate. But I don't know *how* he made the connection."

"Visions are not my field. It's never happened to me before, or to anyone I've hypnotized." Samuel bowed his head and grasped handfuls of his hair. "Bloody hell. I need to find out more."

"Myer might know," Langley said.

"We asked him if he was the man in our visions, but he wasn't," I said. "I really don't want to return to London to ask him more questions." Nor did I want Samuel to. I felt safer with him near me.

"Nobody has to go to London. Myer's coming here, tomorrow."

"What?" Samuel exploded. "Why?"

"He wants to study our ruins. Apparently he's got an interest in archaeology."

We all stared at him. "You want that man *here*?" Samuel growled. "After what he did?"

"He summoned a demon on our property, Uncle!" Sylvia cried. "He cannot be trusted."

"He won't try that again. He admitted he made a mistake. I believe he has learned his lesson."

Samuel approached Langley. He towered over the figure in the wheelchair, but Langley didn't flinch away. Samuel's fists closed at his sides and his hair stuck out at odd angles from when he'd bunched it. Bollard stepped around the wheelchair to stand between his master and Samuel. The muscles in his usually blank face tensed and the lines around his mouth deepened.

Samuel did not back down, nor did he advance. "I don't understand," he said, voice low and harsh. "You're allowing someone of dubious character to come and stay with us?"

"Not stay. He'll get rooms in the village. He's free to come and go to the ruins, but that's all."

"Bollard?" Samuel said. "You agree with this?"

The tension left Bollard's shoulders, but he did not step back to his position behind the wheelchair. He gave Samuel a doubtful look then signed something with his hands.

"Ah, I see," Samuel said with a sneer. "Bollard claims that we're getting something in return," he told me. "What is it, August? It can't be money. What does Myer have that you want?"

"Knowledge. And it's not just me who will benefit from his knowledge, Samuel. You will too. He's going to help us with our experiments. Perhaps soon I will be able to give you what you want."

His gaze flicked to mine as he said it. I sat there, stunned, wondering what in the world their experiments had to do with me. I did not get a chance to ask. Bollard wheeled Langley out of the room, and Samuel also departed.

I was left with Sylvia and our cups of tea, like two ladies of impeccable character with no say whatsoever in the affairs of men. The first part may not have been true, but the truth of the second stung.

CHAPTER 8

"Are you sure you don't mind associating with the likes of me, Miss Charity?" Tommy's smirk softened his criticism, but I still felt the sting of it.

"Don't, Tommy. I feel guilty enough that I'm sleeping in a comfortable bed in a guest room when you're confined to the servants' quarters."

"The servants' quarters are comfortable, too. And you have no need to feel guilty. I like my job. It's good work and keeps me out of mischief." He winked. "The other staff are friendly, and Jack's a good master."

I pulled a face. "Doesn't it gall you to think of him as your m-master?" The last word tripped on my tongue, but I would not dwell on it. Our conversation had nothing to do with the horrible business that had sent me fleeing to Frakingham.

We sat at the large kitchen table used by the servants to prepare food. Mrs. Moore also sat with us, needle and thread in hand, bent over a shirt. If she were listening in on our conversation, she gave no indication. She hadn't approved of my joining Tommy in the service area. The scowl she directed at me as I entered was rather a giveaway and her added comment about the lateness of the hour was another.

It was almost ten o'clock. Sylvia had already retired for the night and Samuel was with Langley in his laboratory. I'd sought out my friend to avoid the loneliness, and my own tumultuous thoughts.

I ignored Mrs. Moore's disapproving looks and accepted Tommy's offer of a cup of chocolate. He made it at the stove, expertly whipping it to a froth, then served it to me in one of the cups used by the servants.

"Not at all," Tommy said with that mischievous smirk of his. He was always the jovial one, never seeming to take life too seriously, which was why I liked him so much. In a world full of trials, his presence lifted my spirits. "Jack doesn't treat me that way. It's mostly the way it was in the old days between us."

"I'm glad to hear it. But what about the other Langleys?"

"What about them?"

"Do they accept you as being, well, more than a servant?"

"Charity, I'm not more than a servant here."

"You are! You're Jack's friend. I do hope they don't ignore you or take you for granted."

Mrs. Moore pushed back her chair and shot to her feet. She glared at me, then spun around and strode out the door. What had I said to upset her so?

"The Langleys aren't like that," Tommy said.

"Sylvia is."

"No, she's not. She can be all bluster and steam at times, but she's got a kind heart underneath that crisp façade." His smile softened, confirming my suspicion. He was indeed sweet on her.

I sipped my chocolate and watched him over the rim of my cup. He seemed lost in thought for a moment, his gaze distant. "Tommy," I hedged, setting the cup down. "Be careful with these people. I don't mean Jack, I mean the other Langleys."

He cocked his head to the side. I had his full attention.

"You and I both know August Langley is not Jack's real uncle," I went on. "He could disown Jack whenever he wishes and throw him out of Frakingham."

He snorted. "He won't do that."

"What if Jack does something disagreeable?"

"He wouldn't."

"You don't know that. Jack's loyal to his friends and Mr. Langley is, well, he's a toff."

He picked up his cup and held it tightly between both hands. "You think I'll give Jack cause to make a choice between supporting Langley and supporting me." He did not deny that Langley was a toff, or that he cared about appearances and maintaining a sense of class within the household. He didn't deny any of it.

"It might never come to that," I said, choosing my words carefully. "It doesn't have to."

"Is there somefin' spiffic you want to tell me?" he said in his London slum accent of our childhood. "Forgive me poor, slow brain but I don't know what you're tryin' to tell me."

I sighed. "Calm down, Tommy. I'm merely suggesting that you stop flirting with Sylvia. Her uncle doesn't seem aware of it yet, but it's only a matter of time. If he finds out, he might dismiss you. Jack would naturally defend you and, well, relations between the members of the family will become strained."

"Our business don't concern you, Charity."

"It does where Jack is concerned. Don't jeopardize what he has here."

"How 'bout you leave Jackie alone now he's wed. He don't need the likes o' you remindin' him o' past mistakes."

I bristled. My grip tightened on my cup. I fought against the urge to throw its contents over him. Despite our argument, he was my friend. We'd fought like this in the old days—Jack too—but this was the first time in recent years that we'd said such cruel things to one another. Yet I didn't want to give in to my anger, no matter how much his words stung. What he was doing was wrong. It not only threatened his and Jack's position, but it would confuse poor Sylvia. She wasn't like me; she didn't have any defences against flirtatious men. There was a danger she would take him seriously and ruin herself.

"Sylvia is young, innocent, and you're... well, you're far more experienced when it comes to relations between men and women."

"I ain't the only one," he mumbled into his cup.

"My past isn't under discussion here. This isn't about me."

He set down the cup and flattened both palms on the table. He leaned towards me. I wasn't afraid, not of Tommy. He and Jack would never hurt me. "No," he ground out. "It's never 'bout you. You always avoided talk of *your* mistakes. You never think 'bout how *your* actions put Jackie in danger. You only want to run away from yourself and forget."

My heart plunged to the floor. A lump of ice took its place in my chest, spreading its cold through me. His words echoed inside my head, making it impossible to think of a retort.

But there was no retort that could change the fact that he was right.

"Sorry," he muttered. "I shouldn't have said that. You don't remember." He looked down at his cup then quickly put it to his lips and sipped.

I may not remember precisely what had happened, but I knew he was right. The guilt was carving out a hole inside me. It would only be there if he was telling the truth.

I slowly stood. It was difficult to maintain balance, with dizziness filling my head and blurring my vision. I steadied myself with a hand on the table then made my way to the door. Somehow Tommy was already there. How odd. I'd not seen him move. Then again, I could see so little through my eyes, clogged with tears as they were.

"I'm sorry," he whispered. His mouth was pulled down and his eyes swam. "I didn't mean any of it. I was angry and… and I'm sorry." The slum accent had disappeared—how remarkable that he could switch it on and off.

"There's no need to apologize." I forced a smile. "It's late. I ought to go to bed."

I went to move past him but he stopped me. "Charity." He bowed his head and sucked in a breath. When he looked up again, I was struck by the raw emotion imprinted in every frown line. "It's not what I think at all."

"I know."

"Stop being so reasonable about it." He shook his head sadly. "Get angry with me. Shout at me. You know it's not true, don't you? What I said, it's not—"

I put a finger to his lips to stop him. There really was no other way and he was going to dig an even bigger hole if he kept talking. I opened my mouth to tell him that it was true, but I didn't think he needed to hear it. He looked more upset by his words than I felt.

And I was deeply disturbed by them.

"What is this?" Samuel emerged from the dark shadows of the corridor beyond. He did not carry a candle and the way wasn't lit. He paused some feet away and stared at us, at my finger on Tommy's lips. He blinked hard at me, as if he didn't believe what he was seeing. "Charity?" he murmured.

I lowered my hand to my stomach. I felt ill. As if I did not carry enough guilt already, now he thought Tommy and I were lovers.

"It was nothing. Charity and I were just talking." Tommy's words stumbled over themselves in his eagerness to get them out. "In fact, I was talking too much. I said some things I shouldn't and she was trying to stop me." He dug his hand through his hair and swore under his breath. "Sorry." It wasn't clear whom he was apologizing to.

Samuel did not look at Tommy. He continued to stare at me and I stared back, challenging him to say something, to accuse me of something base. I watched as his lips pressed together and a muscle in his jaw jumped. Slowly, his gaze slid to Tommy. "You should have more of a care, Dawson." His voice was low, ominous, not at all like his usual smooth one.

"Tommy did nothing," I said. "You saw with your own eyes. I was the one touching him. Leave him be."

His nostrils flared. He turned and strode back along the corridor.

"Gladstone!" Tommy called after him. He went to follow, but I grabbed his arm.

"I'll talk to him."

"I don't think that's a good idea."

I ignored him and raced after Samuel. I trailed my hand along the wall to follow its bends in the darkness until finally I emerged into the lamp-lit corridor that led to the main part of the house.

"Samuel, wait!"

I found him at the base of the grand staircase in the entrance hall. He stood with one hand on the spherical cap of the newel post, his chest rising and falling heavily.

"Don't try to protect him, Charity. I saw the intimacy between the two of you, and I am not merely referring to your touching him."

Men are blind and stupid, even the clever ones with exceptional eyesight. "Don't be absurd. You're acting the fool. There is nothing between Tommy and I, except long-time friendship. There never has been anything more."

"Nevertheless—" He cut himself off. His fingers flexed around the newel post. "Nevertheless, Tommy should have more of a care."

I rolled my eyes, but he wasn't looking at me and my frustration was lost on him. I moved to where I could see his face. "For goodness' sake. Believe us or not, I don't care. Neither of us owes you an explanation."

"You are here under my care! Under Langley's!"

I gave a bitter laugh. "You can't possibly be talking about protecting my reputation. That's absurd. I know you know about Jack and me."

He went rigid. "That doesn't mean I don't want to protect you!"

"From Tommy? It's not me you need to protect, where he's concerned."

He lifted his gaze to mine for the first time. "What do you mean?"

"Sylvia is more in danger of buckling under Tommy's charm than I. You know how it is between them. You told me about their affection yourself."

"That is merely flirting. They're unsuitable and nothing can come of it. Whereas you… you and Tommy…"

"Ah, yes." I lifted my chin and met his gaze. "I'm more Tommy's *sort*, aren't I? The loose girl from the rookery and her servant lover. What a fine match we make."

He slammed his palm down hard on the newel post. "That's not what I mean!"

I flinched and backed away, my heart tripping over itself in fright. *Oh God, oh God.*

I had to get away, go somewhere safe. Alone. I gathered up my skirts and raced up the stairs.

He followed me. "Charity! Wait! I'm sorry, I—"

"Do *not* follow me," I growled. "Do not come anywhere near me."

My last vision was not of him, but of myself. I was looking through his eyes, seeing my own flushed face, my heaving chest. I dropped my skirts and put a hand out to the balustrade for balance.

Just as quickly, the vision vanished again. I picked up my skirts once more and raced up the stairs, but not before I saw the sorrow in Samuel's swirling eyes.

***

I did not go to my room. I continued up the stairs, snatching a candle from the table on the landing as I passed. I continued up, past the attic to the narrow spiral staircase leading to the sitting room at the top of one of the towers. It was a cozy space with a chaise tucked beneath the window, from which I could watch the night sky. One couldn't see so many stars in London.

I blew out the candle and sat in the dark. I felt like one of the stars, shining my light down on the world. It was humbling yet uplifting too, affirming that my little light was as important as any other.

The problem with feeling calm again was that I regretted my flight. I should have remained and spoken to Samuel, helped him see reason. When my temper had flared, so had his. Yet I got the distinct impression that he wasn't able to control his temper like he usually could. It was almost as if he wasn't used to it and didn't know how.

Nevertheless, I shouldn't have fled. The look on his face had distressed me more than his angry outburst. I wished, with a heavy heart, to go to him and check if he was all right.

I got my wish when he opened the door to the little tower room. There were no signs of his earlier temper. Indeed, he looked relieved.

"I've searched everywhere for you." He set his candle down on the table between my chaise and the bookcase. The flame swayed in the draft coming through the door, and reflected in his dark eyes.

"Samuel, I'm sorry. I shouldn't have run off."

He sat in the armchair and leaned forward, his elbows resting on his knees. "I don't blame you for it. For any of this." He heaved a deep sigh and bowed his head. "I shouldn't have spoken to you that way, or to Tommy. Now that I've calmed down, my head can see what my heart couldn't."

His heart?

My own skipped a beat. "Samuel, there is no blame here. But you must understand that I am a grown woman, with no kin and no intention of marrying."

He looked up and frowned. "Why not?"

The poor man. He really didn't understand. I supposed he rarely encountered unconventional females. "Why would I swap good employment where I can come and go as I please to be a decorative ornament at best, or a drudge at worst? I like my life at the school. It's fulfilling. I see no reason to throw it away."

"What about children?"

"I have children at the orphanage. Dozens of them. In many ways, I am their parent."

"It's not the same."

"How do you know?"

He sighed. "Very well, what about love, then?"

I smiled gently. "That's sweet of you to suggest the possibility, but I am not so naive to think it would come my way now, after the life I've led." The truth of that hit me in the throat. I was aware that I wanted to experience love again, after my bleak memories had been blocked, but I knew now that it was unlikely, given my situation. Besides, I had the love of the children and loved them in return. It was fulfilling in every way. Yes. Most fulfilling.

He sat back in the chair as if I'd pushed him in the chest. "I... I had not expected this."

I shrugged one shoulder. "So you see, my reputation is in no danger. I don't need protecting."

"Then why flee to Frakingham?"

"That's different and you know it. My freedom was at stake at the orphanage, perhaps my life." I felt my blood pumping again, fueling my temper. Why did we disagree now? We had never done so before he put the memory block in place. "Don't twist this situation to suit your own argument, Samuel."

"I have no argument. I have no motive."

Bollocks. Of course he did. All men had a motive where women were concerned. "Let's not discuss this further. It's only going to end in us fighting, and I'm tired of fighting with you."

"I don't want to fight with you either." He gave me a grim smile. "I'm sorry, Charity. I seem to be more forthright lately. Something's come over me..." He trailed off and looked away.

We both knew what had come over him. My memories. *You only want to run away from yourself and forget.*

I tried to block out Tommy's words, but they ate at me like a cancer.

"What's that?" Samuel rose out of his chair and peered over my head at the window.

I followed his gaze and saw something, far below, in the distance. A small light glowed in the direction of the ruins. It darted upwards and moved back and forth, before dipping low again. It wasn't a flame, but it wasn't a sharp, bright light, either.

"What is it?" I asked.

"Someone's down there."

"Who would creep around the ruins at night? If it were a visitor, they'd come via the drive, surely."

His gaze connected with mine. He did not need to tell me what he was thinking, because it had crossed my mind too—the intruder at the school had found me here, and was coming for me.

Cold fingers tightened their grip on my throat. I clutched the side of the chaise for balance.

Samuel picked up his candle and headed out of the tower room. I followed him down the stairs to the kitchen, where Tommy still sat. "Fetch a lamp," Samuel ordered him. "Come with me. Someone is lurking in the ruins."

"Bloody hell," Tommy muttered.

Samuel clapped him on the shoulder as Tommy lifted the lamp off the hook near the door. It would seem their earlier argument was forgotten.

I followed them to the service door near the scullery, but hung back.

"I thought you might insist upon coming," Samuel said, with a smirk that looked decidedly wicked with the candlelight flickering beneath his chin.

"I'm not a fool," I said.

Tommy snorted. "But you are stubborn."

"Are you two quite finished?"

Samuel handed me his candle, his expression once more serious. "Lock the door after we leave and only open it at the sound of my voice, or Tommy's."

I took the candlestick. My fingers brushed his, sending a wash of tingles shooting across my skin. Our gazes met. His was smoky, warm.

"Be careful," I said. "If it is that man, he's very strong."

He nodded. Of course he knew the fellow. Knew how much of a monster he was. He grabbed a knife from a drawer.

They shut the door and I returned to the tower room for a better view. The house was quiet. All external doors were locked, yet my heart still felt like it was going to choke me.

I settled onto the chaise and watched Tommy's lamp move across the lawn. The other still bobbed around the ruins of the old abbey. The crescent moon's reflection glistened like an ethereal water serpent on the lake's surface. Along with Tommy's lamp, it provided enough light for me to see the dark figures of my friends, but not the intruder further away.

I hadn't yet explored the ruins, only seen them from the house. In daylight it seemed quite a pretty, if ethereal, place. I imagined that visiting it during the night would be more unnerving, particularly with someone unknown wandering about.

Suddenly, Tommy's light took off at speed towards the ruins. The other light hovered in mid-air for a moment, then it moved quickly away, bobbing madly.

I blew out a breath. It was a good sign that the trespasser was running and not confronting Tommy and Samuel. Either he was harmless, his intentions innocent, or he knew he couldn't win against two strong young men, which ruled out the brute doing his master's bidding.

I headed back downstairs, but had to pause on the second floor landing as a vision took over. I was looking through Samuel's eyes again, into the blurred light of a lamp. It was too bright and close for me to make out the figure holding it. Tommy's face came into view then. He seemed to be talking to me—Samuel—but I couldn't hear his words.

The vision cleared and I was once more in the house. I continued on down the stairs and waited at the service door until I heard Samuel softly call my name. I opened the door and Tommy came through first, followed by—

Everett Myer!

He bowed upon seeing me. "Ah, now this welcoming party is far more appealing. I didn't know you were here at Frakingham, Miss Evans." He straightened and smiled. "I apologize for the disturbance at such a late hour. I had expected to slip in and slip away quietly, but it would seem your friends are vigilant."

Samuel moved past him, bumping him in the shoulder. "We have need to be."

"Ah yes, Freak House, the villagers call this place. I suspect the local youths like to sneak about the grounds to impress their friends."

Samuel blinked at him. "No," was all he said. He looked quite different to when he'd left me. His hair stuck out like he'd been pulling at it, and deep grooves ran the length of his forehead. He dragged the back of his hand across his mouth and did not meet my gaze.

"What are you doing here, Mr. Myer?" I asked. "Mr. Langley said you weren't coming until tomorrow."

"I arrived late today and thought I would investigate the ruins immediately. Darkness brings out the magic in a place like that, and where there's magic, the paranormal is not far away."

Magic, paranormal. If I'd not seen Cara talk to ghosts, or Jack light fires with his hands, I would have thought Myer a madman. But I knew about the things they'd encountered before Christmas. It made me more impressed by Samuel and Tommy's bravery at venturing outside into the night.

"Besides," Myer said. "I'm loath to waste time. It's taken much petitioning to get Mr. Langley to agree to me researching his ruins, and I don't want to waste a moment of this unexpected opportunity."

"Then you shouldn't creep around at night," Samuel snapped. "He can take away what's been given."

Myer's face fell. "I pray you don't tell him, Gladstone."

Once again Samuel dragged his hand through his hair. He seemed to be in turmoil, and I didn't think it had anything to do with finding Myer.

I touched his shoulder and the muscles corded. "What is it?"

He didn't answer.

I glanced at Tommy, but he merely shrugged. "Was it the vision?" I asked.

Still no verbal answer from Samuel, but his muscles tensed more. A vein popped out in his neck above his collar. "What did you see?" I whispered.

A single shake of his bowed head. He closed his eyes and breathed deeply. Whatever he'd seen had disturbed him. He couldn't have seen through my eyes then, but the other man's. The master.

"Did you see a woman?" I asked him.

"Stop," he hissed. "I cannot answer you."

Cannot or would not? I suspected it was the latter. I also suspected I was right and he'd seen the same girl I'd seen when I looked through that man's eyes. A frightened girl in a bedroom.

She didn't belong there.

I didn't know where that thought had come from, or why I'd thought it, but I knew I was right. A sickening feeling congealed in my gut. Oh God. We had to help her.

"Charity?" Tommy asked. "Are you all right?"

I shook my head. "Not really." I answered him, but I looked at Myer. "You see, Samuel and I had a vision just now. I saw through his eyes and he saw through the other man's."

"The same fellow you told me about?" Myer asked.

"I believe so. You see, there have been some developments, since we last spoke with you. It explains my reason for being here." I told him about my attempted kidnapping and the man who'd been behind those attacks—a man named the master who seemed to know me personally. A man who I'd seen die.

"So, you see the problem," I said. "We cannot give the police directions or even a description of this so-called master. He doesn't exist."

He leaned back against the scullery bench and held up the lantern to my face. He studied me for some time, then looked to both Tommy and Samuel. "I can see how you would think he doesn't exist, Miss Evans. After all, you have little experience with the supernatural."

Samuel's head snapped up. "What sort of supernatural are you talking about?"

"Ghosts."

I shook my head. "I've seen Cara—Miss Moreau—talk to ghosts, but I haven't been able to see them. I concede that perhaps I might be able to see through the eyes of one, but I don't believe this master is a spirit. There's another girl in my visions, you see, and *she* can see him. I'm quite certain of it. Unless you think she's a medium?"

"I doubt it. I would have heard about her. And anyway, you've missed the point. Ghosts are only visible to mediums when in ghost form. They become as real as you and me when they take over a living body."

"Possession," Samuel murmured. "The master's ghost has possessed someone."

I gasped.

"But why?" Tommy asked. "Why not go up to Heaven or… the other place."

"The fact he hasn't passed over means he's restless," Myer said. "He has something unresolved that he needs to do on this realm."

"Me," I murmured. "I am his unresolved business."

The room closed in. My breaths came in rapid bursts, yet I couldn't fill my lungs. Couldn't think through the fog inside my head. Everything tilted and I lost my balance. I reached out for the nearest thing—Samuel.

"Charity?" He scooped his arm around my waist just in time to catch me as I fainted.

CHAPTER 9

I awoke in the bed I'd been using since my arrival at Frakingham. Light edged the velvet curtains and brightened the room a little. It was morning.

"Ah," said a man I didn't recognize. "You're awake." The pink lips peeping out between gray moustache and beard smiled in a benignly polite way. He leaned forward and peered into my eyes.

"Thank goodness!" Sylvia came into view beside him. She clasped my hand, resting on top of the bedcovers. "We were so worried, but Dr. Gowan said you would be well enough after a sound sleep."

"What happened?" I asked.

"You fainted from exhaustion," the doctor said.

"Exhaustion? But I didn't feel particularly tired."

"From worry then, after which you merely fell asleep." He nodded and murmured under his breath then straightened. "Fetch me if there's any change," he told Sylvia. "I suspect she'll reach a full recovery very soon. It was merely a nervous condition."

"Nervous condition?" I struggled to sit up. Sylvia tried to stop me, but I pushed her hand away. "I do not suffer from nerves, doctor."

"Ah, well," was all he said. He picked a black bag up off the floor. "Get some rest, Miss Evans. Do not frighten the good people of Frakingham any more than you already have."

I watched him leave then looked to Sylvia. Had I really worried her and the others? She did indeed seem concerned. I shouldn't be surprised; I'd fainted in her house. Me, a usually robust and healthy individual.

Then I recalled *why* I'd fainted. The master's ghost had possessed someone, and was now after me.

I gripped Sylvia's hand hard. She winced. "Your strength has returned, I see."

I apologized and let her go.

"I am pleased you're going to be well again," she said in earnest. "I received quite a fright when Tommy woke me last night to tell me you'd fainted."

Her kindly words surprised me. They held none of the coolness she'd directed toward me since my arrival. Perhaps her concern had broken through the barrier she'd erected between us. I was beginning to see why Hannah liked her, now. She could be quite sweet.

I tried to recall the events of the evening. I'd collapsed in the scullery surrounded by Samuel, Tommy and Myer. Samuel had caught me. Had he carried me to the bed too? I checked under the covers. I wore only a nightgown.

"Maud helped me undress you," Sylvia said. "You were quite asleep. Tommy went to fetch the doctor immediately. This was his second visit. It's mid-morning."

"Goodness. How could I have slept so long?"

She shrugged. "Perhaps it was exhaustion, like he said, brought on by shock. Tommy said you got quite the scare when Mr. Myer showed up. I can't blame you. I would have been terrified out of my wits too, to see someone walking in our ruins after dark. That place is frightful even during the day! And that man is…" She shuddered. "I don't trust him."

It would seem Tommy hadn't told her what Myer had said about possession. Perhaps it was best she didn't know.

She was a nervous girl. It would seem I was more the nervous sort than I had realized, too.

I threw the covers off and swung my legs out of the bed.

"What are you doing?" Sylvia cried. She grabbed hold of my legs and swung them back. I was caught so unawares that I didn't resist.

"I'm getting up."

"You mustn't, unless it's to use the privy. Do you need to go?"

"No. Actually, I'm hungry." I swung my legs out again.

She pushed them back, giving me a glare. "Stay in bed."

"I didn't hear the doctor say I had to remain abed any longer."

"He did say to rest."

"Rest, not *bed* rest."

She clicked her tongue. "Nevertheless, I think you should stay here and let me take care of you. I'm quite a good nurse, ask Tommy. Now, stay here and I'll have some breakfast sent up. Then I'll read to you."

Spare me. She might be the best nurse in the world, but bed rest was so dull. "Actually, I need to speak to Samuel."

"You can't." She settled the bedcovers around my hips, tucking them in as if that could trap me. "It's not proper for him to see you in bed."

"That's why I want to get up!"

She clicked her tongue. "Stay here. I'll be back in a moment with some dry toast."

"Dry toast? Can't I have it with butter and marmalade? Oh and some eggs and bacon too, please."

"No." She gave an emphatic shake of her head. "Dry toast only. It's better for the stomach."

"My stomach is fine."

She left without making further comment, although her glare was sharp enough to pin me to the bed.

I got up and donned my gray dress. It was a plain gown, like all of my clothes, with none of the pretty embellishments like Sylvia's. It was well made, however, and had served me two years already without needing any mending. Perhaps I could add some ribbon or lace to it.

I checked myself in the dressing table mirror and sighed. My cheeks did look a little pale. I pinched them, but it did little to improve their color.

I left the bedroom and went in search of Samuel. I found him coming out of August Langley's laboratory, on the top floor, in a part of the house that had suffered damage in the fire. The restoration was so good that it was impossible to tell where the new started and the old ended. I thought it odd that a wheelchair bound man would have his rooms so high in the house, but I supposed it didn't matter overmuch when one was reclusive. Bollard must carry him up and down when necessary.

I peeked through the door as Samuel opened it and got a view of a long room that seemed to run half the length of the eastern wing. There were overflowing bookshelves, chests of drawers, and large tables cluttered with papers and instruments. There were glass jars filled with liquids and things I couldn't identify from my position. Some pretty paintings lined the walls and an armchair near the window looked out at the scenery. It was all rather normal for a science laboratory, until one looked down at the far end, past the tables.

Bollard stood near a large wooden chair that resembled a throne more than a mere chair. It was huge, with an intricately carved back and arm rests. The back came up to Bollard's chin and he was not a small man. Metal pipes and coils sprang from behind it and reached through the slats like mechanical tentacles. It was difficult to tell whether they were attached to the chair or a contraption behind. The servant fiddled with the knobs on a box nearby, while Langley studied a piece of paper. I couldn't fathom what a microbiologist needed with a hideous piece of furniture like that. I thought his tools of trade consisted of microscopes, syringes and glass dishes.

"Are you well, Charity?" Samuel asked. He closed the door behind him, shutting off my view of the laboratory.

"Yes, thank you. And thank you for seeing that I got to my room last night." I felt my face heat at the thought of Samuel holding me. I didn't know why. I'd had men hold me before, and far more intimately, yet never blushed at the thought of it.

"My pleasure," he said. "Uh, I don't mean pleasure, I mean... I was glad I was there to catch you." He blushed fiercely and chewed on his lower lip.

I suppressed a giggle. It was sweet to see such a confident gentleman as Samuel stumble, but I didn't want to make him feel awkward. "I don't know what came over me."

"Shock, I suspect."

"I am usually not as shockable as that."

He frowned. "The last few days have been draining on me, I can only guess how it has been for you."

We walked slowly together down the stairs. I wasn't quite sure where we were heading, but he seemed as content as I was to just walk.

"Samuel, we need to talk about our visions and—"

"No, Charity, we don't."

"Samuel, please. It's—"

"No!" He quickened his pace.

"Slow down," I said, trying to keep up. "Do you wish me to faint again?" It was perhaps a low thing to say, since I didn't feel at all dizzy. But it did get him to pause and wait for me.

He kept his head bowed and didn't look at me. Blond strands of his hair hung over his eyes, obscuring them.

"Are you all right?" he asked, peeking out through the wisps of hair.

I nodded. "I am on the road to recovery, but I have a suspicion that I cannot fully recover until my mind is at ease."

"You're not getting your memory back, then. It won't help ease your mind in the least."

"Actually, I wasn't going to ask you to remove the block."

He lifted his chin to look at me properly. "Oh? Then what?"

"I want to find that girl. The one in our visions. I'm worried about her."

"What makes you think she's in danger?"

"You."

"Me? What have I said?"

"It wasn't what you said, but your reaction last night. You were deeply troubled when you came inside, and I doubted it had anything to do with catching Myer. It had to be from the vision. Since I saw that girl during my last vision, through that man's eyes, I suspect you saw her this time, too. What did she look like?"

He shook his head. "I don't want to discuss this with you." He set off down the stairs again, albeit it at a slower pace.

"Why not?"

"I just don't. Accept it." The sweetness of a few moments before had completely vanished, once again, with the harsh directness of his words. Much like the character in *The Strange Case of Dr. Jekyll and Mr. Hyde*, it was as if he were two distinct people.

I followed him in silence until we reached the bottom of the staircase in the entrance hall. "Are you worried that discussing it will trigger my own memories?" I said quietly. I hardly knew what I was saying. The words seemed to tumble out on their own.

"There's a distinct possibility that it will," he said. "I won't risk that. You cannot have the memory unblocked."

"Cannot? What if I want it back? It is my memory."

"You just told me you didn't want it."

"That's not the point. The point is that you should allow it if that were my wish."

He shook his head and strode off to the front door. "You're not getting it back."

I chased after him. "You can't make the decision on my behalf."

"Yes, I can." He crossed the lawn in the direction of the ruins and lake. It was a sunny day, so while leaving without hat, coat and gloves may have been unconventional, at least we wouldn't get cold.

I picked up my skirts and walked at a brisk pace to keep up. Or perhaps it would be more accurate to say that I stomped after him in exasperation. The effect was lost, however, on the soft grass. "I ought to have the right to decide, not you."

"No, you shouldn't." He stopped suddenly and rounded on me. Cold fury glinted in his eyes. "You don't know what that memory contains. I do. Only I can make a decision in your best interests."

"My best interests!" I threw up my hands, letting my skirts go. They swayed around my ankle boots before settling. "Need I remind you that you have no authority over me? I make my own decisions—"

"So you like to remind me," he ground out. He strode off again.

I followed but said nothing. Anger simmered inside me for several paces, but then I made a conscious decision to let it go. Our argument was pointless, since I didn't want to remember again. What I did want was to help that girl.

"Samuel, wait. Please, we have to talk about her. I have a terrible foreboding about her situation."

That got him stopping and turning to face me once more. "You've remembered something?"

"Not exactly. It's more of a feeling."

He blew out a measured breath. "Go on."

"I get them sometimes, these feelings. I will inexplicably become afraid, or I get the sensation of being closed in or trapped. I think it's related to my blocked memory."

He said nothing, confirming my suspicion.

"I feel anxious for her and I can't really explain why. She looked frightened in my vision. How did she look in yours?"

He didn't answer for a long time. When he did, his voice was soft, hesitant. "Like a young woman who could be anybody, anywhere. There was no indication that she was in trouble. I saw no… signs of distress, except for a few tears."

"The signs could be on her back." Like mine.

"The truth of the matter is, we don't know, Charity. She might be this fellow's daughter, or even his wife."

"Indeed she might be, but if the master's ghost has possessed someone, say her father, then she could be very much in danger."

"Or he might be doing nothing but scolding her."

"If you really believed that then you would not have looked so worried last night. Nor would you have a concern about returning my memory."

"The two may not be linked."

I rolled my eyes. "Of course they are. It's quite obvious to me and I don't even possess that memory anymore."

He walked off on me again. I sighed and trotted to keep up. "Why won't you help?" I said, drawing alongside him. "At least try to investigate."

"Investigate what? We have no clues. As to why I don't try harder, she is not my responsibility. You are."

"Me?" I stumbled over my own feet. Lightning quick, he caught me before I fell. His thumbs rubbed my elbows in little circles. Despite the fabric of my gown, I could feel the warmth of his skin. His gaze connected with mine for a brief, heart-stopping moment. I saw something in his eyes that I'd seen so many times before in the eyes of men— desire.

But there was something else, too. Something I couldn't identify. Perhaps it was concern; he certainly seemed quite worried about me, enough to consider me his responsibility when he didn't need to.

My chest began to ache. I'd never been anyone's responsibility before. I supposed I had been my mother's, when I was little, but afterward I'd always taken care of myself and made my own decisions. Jack had protected me when I needed it, but he'd never thought of me as his responsibility. No more than the other orphans living in our derelict house.

This was new. I wasn't sure if I liked it or not. Nevertheless, the ache didn't go away.

Samuel let me go. "Sylvia is under my care too, of course," he muttered.

"Yes," I muttered back. "Of course." The woman I'd met at Claridge's came to mind. Did he not consider *her* his responsibility, even though she considered herself engaged to him? Why *had* Samuel put off an engagement to such a beauty? It was most odd, and seemed quite unlike him. Well, unlike the man he used to be before he took my memory.

My thoughts had wandered in an unexpected direction, dampening my frustration. I decided to leave the conversation about the girl in our visions alone for now. There were just too many unknowns. Even if she was in trouble, how would we find her?

"Where are you going, anyway?" I asked him, as he walked off again.

"To see Myer." He nodded at the ruins. "He's down there."

"What happened to him after I fainted?

"Tommy drove him back into the village when he went to fetch the doctor last night."

"Where is he staying?"

"With the mayor and his wife, the Butterworths." He shook his head, his face grim.

"You don't like the Butterworths?"

"I do, but... Myer once confessed that he and Mrs. Butterworth were having a liaison."

I gasped. "That's despicable. Poor Mr. Butterworth and Mrs. Myer."

He nodded. "Precisely. I thought they'd stopped since he hadn't been to the village for some time. It would appear there is still something afoot, however."

I liked the man less and less.

Myer waved at us from where he stood inside a crumbling arch. He looked like a man happy to be precisely where he was, pottering around a scattered pile of old stones.

"I'm very glad to see you up and about, Miss Evans," he said. "You had us concerned, last night."

"I'm well enough today, thank you."

"Here, Gladstone, what do you think of this?" He handed Samuel a wooden rectangular instrument.

"It's a thermometer," I said with a shrug of my shoulders.

Samuel turned it over. "And barometer," he said. "What will these tell you about paranormal patterns?"

"My apologies, I forgot that your theoretical knowledge of the supernatural is limited."

"My practical knowledge is bloody excellent," Samuel said, not apologizing for his foul language. "I have vast experience at sending demons back, for example."

If Myer felt the barb, he gave no indication. He seemed excited by his instruments, like a schoolboy in one of my own science classes, discovering how to make baking powder fizz.

"The temperature in these ruins is marginally lower than just outside," he said.

"You probably should allow for some inaccuracy in your instrument," Samuel said.

Myer waved his suggestion off. "The really exciting thing is the reading from the barometer. The atmospheric pressure inside these ruins is low. Outside, the reading is normal. Such extreme changes in a relatively small area are not possible."

"Meaning?" I prompted.

"Studies by society members have shown that the low temperature of an area, relative to the external temperature, is conducive to a higher concentration of supernatural activity. I believe that supernatural energy is playing havoc with the barometer, giving false readings."

"Do you mean there are more ghosts hereabouts?" I asked, looking around. Aside from some rather picturesque, moss-covered arches, broken walls and scattered stones, the ruins didn't look different to any other ruin. I did like it, though. It would be quite peaceful to sit against a stone and watch the sun sink over the horizon.

"Ghosts, demons and other creatures," Myer said.

"Demons?" Ghosts didn't particularly worry me, but demons did, after hearing about the terrible time Hannah and Jack had with them at Christmas.

"That's enough, Myer," Samuel said, his voice low. "There's no need to mention such things."

"My apologies." Myer bowed to me. "You have a delicate constitution. You shouldn't be frightened."

"I most certainly do not have a delicate constitution."

Beside me, Samuel smothered a chuckle, but not very well. I shot him a glare and he stopped smiling.

"My constitution is very strong," I told Myer. "Usually. You mentioned other creatures are attracted to these ruins. What other creatures are you referring to?"

"Fairies, angels, beasts that have been relegated to mere mythological status of late." He shrugged one shoulder. "All manner of things."

"Good lord. And what is it they come here to do?"

"I don't know, yet. I do know that this is an area that attracts them. Whether they're more likely to emerge from here, or just visit from time to time, I can't be sure yet. That's what I hope to discover."

"These creatures are not tourists, Myer," Samuel said. "In fact, I refute your theory altogether. If they were attracted to these ruins, we would know about it. Frakingham would be overrun by creatures."

"Yes," Myer murmured. "I've wondered the same thing. Are you sure you haven't seen any strange beasts running around since those demons were destroyed?"

"Only you."

Myer gave a tight smile. "Very amusing."

"The Langleys have lived here for years and they've not mentioned it. I think an excess of demons or angels is something they would have noticed and thought worth mentioning."

"Hmmm." He took the instrument back and studied the barometer. "It's most unusual."

"What made you think to look here in the first place?" I asked.

"Rumors among my fellow society members, mostly. Some have long suspected there were strong supernatural forces centered here. They've cited texts that mention odd behavior among visitors and residents alike."

"Perhaps those are referencing the ghosts of the little children who occupied the dungeon of the old house until recently," Samuel said.

Myer shook his head. "This is more specific to the ruins. In fact, some of the references date back to when the abbey was still here. There are reports of rituals being conducted within the abbey walls."

It was all giving me a terrible feeling in my gut. I didn't like to think of sinister things happening in such a pretty place. Indeed, it seemed impossible.

"Perhaps the rumors and reports refer back to a time when the abbey was still in use," Samuel said. "I imagine that once it crumbled, it lost some of the so-called magic you speak of."

"The reports persisted through the centuries. And look at these readings! I have pages of them in my notes." He indicated a notebook perched on a wall, the pages curling in the breeze.

"Why are the other society members not helping you with your research?" I asked.

"Langley insisted on me being the only one."

"Because he wishes to gather information from you for his own work?"

He glanced at Samuel then gave me a smooth smile. "I believe so, but I haven't spoken to him about it yet. We have an appointment for later today." He spread out his arms to encompass the ruins surrounding us. "What do you two think? Can you feel the different energy down here?"

"I feel nothing," Samuel said, rather shortly.

"It's a pretty spot." I gazed at the lake. The surface sparkled in the sunlight against a backdrop of greenery. Weeping willows dipped into the water's edge and a fat mother duck paddled lazily as her ducklings trailed behind her. "I certainly feel more at peace here. It's hard to imagine the things you speak of happening."

"Indeed."

"Mr. Myer, can you spare a few minutes to tell us about possession? We didn't have a chance to finish our discussion last night."

He indicated I should sit on a low wall. I did and he sat beside me while Samuel remained standing. "I don't have any personal experience with possession or ghosts, but I'll tell you what I know. If you require first-hand knowledge, I suggest you speak to your friends, the Beauforts."

"Miss Moreau has told me how she communicates with ghosts. She said that she can touch them, but others cannot. They're also limited to the place where they died and cannot move around freely."

"Unless they possess a living body," he said. "A ghost can choose to haunt the place where it died, or move on to the Otherworld. Spirits with unresolved problems will usually remain. It appears that the ghosts who choose to haunt are either angry individuals, who wish to punish the living, or were victims of heinous crimes perpetrated on them in life and wish to haunt their tormentor. By possessing a living person, they become tangible again and can inflict injury if they wish. And since the sort of ghost who haunts is often angered by how they were treated in life, then you can imagine what they would do once they found themselves in control of another's body. Possession is associated with evil for a good reason."

I shuddered. It all sounded so terrible. Samuel skimmed his fingers lightly across my shoulder and I found the simple touch reassuring.

"You have every right to be worried, Miss Evans. It's not easy to remove a spirit once it possesses. Indeed, only a spirit medium can do it, and they must get very near the possessed."

"We need Mrs. Beaufort and Cara's help," I muttered.

Samuel's hand squeezed. "We'll send a telegram immediately." He turned to Myer. "Why is possession so uncommon? Mrs. Beaufort tells me she and Miss Moreau are kept busy assisting unhappy spirits to cross over. If there are so many unhappy spirits, there should be an abundance of possessions."

Myer's face clouded and his lips flattened. "It's not easy for ghosts to possess. Indeed, they have to be summoned into the body. They cannot do it alone."

Samuel's breath hitched. "But only mediums can summon spirits."

"Precisely."

"No," I said. "I don't believe Cara or Mrs. Beaufort would do that."

"Could it happen accidentally?" Samuel asked.

Myer shook his head. His sharp gaze connected with mine. "There are specific words that trigger it. One of them must have spoken them."

"Or there's another spirit medium. One that nobody knows about, who is intent on causing chaos."

CHAPTER 10

The existence of a third spirit medium certainly seemed the most likely explanation. According to Cara, all mediums were descendants of a lost African tribe. In essence, they were all relatives, but they had been scattered across the world through the centuries after white man almost destroyed the tribe. Only women could be mediums, but the ability was passed down the male line. Their number was unknown.

"If there were a third, I'm sure I would be aware of her presence here in England," Myer said.

Samuel's eyes darkened ominously. "Are you suggesting that Emily or Cara are responsible? Careful, Myer. Be very careful."

Myer held up his hands. "I am merely stating facts. Here's another fact for you, Gladstone. Did you know that Miss Cara Moreau once summoned the spirit of a murderer into a body?"

"That doesn't mean she would do it again!" Samuel exploded.

I rested my hand on his arm. My touch seemed to work, because he calmed a little. "When did this happen?" I asked Myer.

"Some years ago."

"Well then, she must have been too young to know what she was doing." I refused to believe that my friend would summon an evil spirit on purpose. She was much too good-natured to do such a thing. "We need to focus our energies on finding this other medium. If we find her, she can tell us whose body she summoned the spirit into."

"If she wants to," Samuel said. "It's likely she won't."

"She could be difficult to find," Myer said. "Indeed, she may have even left the country altogether. Theoretically, a spirit could possess a body indefinitely. I have no knowledge of long-term possession, however, so it remains theory only at this stage."

"If the spirit of the master possessed someone months or even years ago, she could indeed have disappeared." The slim hope I'd momentarily clutched was dashed. We were back to where we began. Nowhere.

"Isn't it likely that it happened recently?" Samuel asked. "It's only now that he's come for Charity, after all."

Myer shook his head. "Perhaps that's only because the visions connecting you three have begun. He must have identified you and your location from the visions, Miss Evans."

Something I'd been wondering about clicked into place. "I think I was looking up at the school's sign when I had a vision on the day of the attempted abduction. That's what made him send his man to the school in the first place."

I shivered again. It was horrible enough knowing someone could see through my eyes, but the fact that he'd found me that way was worse. "Why do you think we have the visions at all? They're terribly inconvenient. Particularly when I don't know when they'll happen."

"Oh, but you do," Myer said. "Think of every time you've had a vision. What is the common factor?"

"At first they happened when we touched," I said, looking at Samuel. "Then it was…"

"When we argued," Samuel finished for me. "One or both of us grew angry or upset. I suspected as much and now you've confirmed my suspicions, Myer. Last night, when I caught you sneaking around down here, I was furious with you."

"I was not sneaking, Gladstone. Merely wandering."

"It's not important," I cut in, before they could clash again. "The important thing is we now know what to do to stop the visions. Remain calm."

Samuel flexed his fingers, as if releasing some tension through them. "I'll try," he said quietly. "It's just that I seem to have a quicker temper now than I used to."

He wasn't looking for an answer, so I didn't tell him it had been that way ever since he'd acquired my memory. I suspected he already knew.

"You may find other triggers," Myer said. "Other heightened emotions could lead to further visions. It will be interesting to conduct an experiment. Perhaps fear or even desire may be factors."

"We are not case studies," I said hotly.

"Aren't you?" He eyed the house. "Have you told August Langley that?"

"What do you mean?"

"Don't listen to him," Samuel snarled. "He's trying to unsettle you."

Then he'd succeeded. August Langley was an odd man, his assistant too. Whatever they were up to in his laboratory, with his chemicals and strange contraptions, had certainly better not involve me. I was no one's experiment.

Myer stood and studied his barometer again. "If you don't mind, I have work to do." He already seemed lost in his own thoughts, our presence and our problems forgotten.

Samuel and I picked our way out of the ruins. When we reached the lawn, he said, "I'll have Tommy go into the village and send a telegram to the Beauforts. They need to be made aware of the third medium, even if there's nothing they can do about her."

"Or about the possession," I said heavily.

His pace slowed and I slowed too. "I'll protect you, Charity. I won't let anyone harm you. You must believe me." His voice was thick and rich. It vibrated across my skin and seeped down into my bones. My head went a little dizzy and I had a ridiculous urge to throw my arms around him.

His head jerked back, as if I'd slapped him. He came to an abrupt halt. "Charity!"

I shook my head and the dizziness vanished. I no longer wanted to grasp him and kiss him all over. Well, actually I did, but not with as much ferocity. How very strange.

I touched my fingers to my temple. "Yes?"

He pressed the heel of his hand to his right eye. "My God, I'm so sorry. I, I didn't know I was doing that."

"Doing what?" And then it struck me. He'd almost hypnotized me. Luckily he'd caught himself before the act was complete, but what if he hadn't? I had succumbed so easily to his lovely voice, his kind manner.

Oh God. My chest tightened. My throat closed. I gasped and gasped again, but it was useless. It was as if the air was too thick to breathe.

"Charity? Charity, what's wrong?"

I couldn't answer him. I bent over, desperate to ease the ache in my chest. My damned corset was too tight! He touched the back of my neck. His hand was warm, solid, reassuring as he rubbed.

And then it was heavy. Too heavy. He was too close. I pushed him away, not hard, but he stumbled back a few steps. I straightened and sucked in air once more.

"Charity?" he whispered. His eyes were wide and unblinking, their depths endless. If I had to guess, I'd say he was frightened.

By my reaction?

Or by what he'd done?

"Is that what August Langley is studying in his laboratory? Your hypnosis? And am I your test subject?"

"No," he whispered through bloodless lips.

My temper grew stronger, now that I could breathe again. "Are you trying to see how easy it is for me to be hypnotized into doing whatever you want?"

"Absolutely not."

"How can I be sure?"

He closed his eyes, and when he opened them again they were softer, yet edged with pain. "Because I already know how easy it is for me to hypnotize you."

My heart dropped like a stone. I was fooling myself if I thought I could trust him. Here was a man who could get people to do whatever he wanted with mere words, a fact I'd almost forgotten. What man could resist such power?

"I am not proud of it," he said. "But I can control it."

"You almost didn't, then."

His brow creased. "Yes," he murmured.

"Why?" I was aware of the heat in my voice, the challenge in my tone. I didn't care. Samuel needed someone to confront him, resist him, and it would seem it would be up to me.

"I don't know," he said. "Charity, please understand that I would never hypnotize you against your wishes. I have no desire to win your affections through false means."

So he wanted to win them through other ones?

I lifted my chin in acknowledgement. Whether he spoke the truth or not, I had to accept his explanation. The fact was, Samuel was the only person I could turn to, and Frakingham House the only safe place for me.

Nevertheless, I would have to be vigilant when he was speaking. As soon as he spoke in *that* voice again, I would leave the room. Or slap him.

We stood there, a little apart, almost like strangers again. No, not quite. Strangers were not as awkward as we were; he could no longer look me in the eyes. My insides twisted suddenly into a knot. Despite what had happened, despite my distrust, I didn't want us to be on unfriendly terms. I didn't want to be a stranger to him. I wanted... what?

I didn't know. All I knew was that if the awkwardness continued, I would be forever sorry.

But I could not think of a single thing to say to him to crack through the ice between us.

Thankfully, a distraction arrived in the form of visitors. A gleaming black coach, pulled by two perfectly matched gray horses, drove along the drive, kicking gravel up beneath its fast moving wheels.

Samuel swore.

"Do you know who it is?" I asked.

"Yes. It's my parents."

***

The maid served our tea. Tommy had been sent into the village by Samuel with a message to telegram the Beauforts, despite the household needing the extra pair of capable hands upon the arrival of Mr. and Mrs. Gladstone.

Sylvia sat primly on the sofa, playing the perfect hostess. She prattled on and offered pastries to her guests, despite receiving only cool refusals in return. I ate four. I was so hungry, having missed breakfast, and Sylvia seemed too preoccupied to remember that I was only supposed to eat dry toast.

"Is Mr. August Langley not at home?" Mrs. Gladstone asked, eyeing the door with caution. She looked as if she'd faint if he walked in, or rolled in as it were.

"He's busy," Samuel said.

Sylvia gave them an apologetic smile. "My uncle rarely ventures out of his rooms. If he were here he would apologize most profusely for, er, himself." She bit her lip and giggled.

I rather suspected she wasn't used to company herself. She didn't seem to know how to behave. The poor girl had probably been sheltered for much of her life if her uncle was her only companion before Jack arrived.

Mrs. Gladstone sipped her tea. Mr. Gladstone stared at his son, who stared right back. There was no awkwardness in his manner now that his temper had returned. The air around him fairly sizzled with his anger.

"Is there somewhere we can speak alone?" Mr. Gladstone asked his son.

Mrs. Gladstone winced at her husband's bluntness. Sylvia blinked down into her teacup. She seemed quite out of her depth. I suspected she'd never had to deal with an authoritative figure like Samuel's father, not without Jack being present.

"Sylvia," I said, "shall we take a turn in the garden?"

"You don't have to go anywhere," Samuel said, his tone steely. "I want you to stay."

"I think it's best if we leave."

I held out my hand to Sylvia and she took it. We walked out of the room without turning back, leaving Samuel and his parents behind, along with our tea and those delicious pastries. Perhaps we could walk to the kitchen instead of the garden.

"Shall we listen in?" she whispered once we were out in the corridor.

"Sylvia! You're so wicked." I grinned. "All right."

We crept back along the wall to the drawing room door. Mrs. Gladstone was speaking in a somewhat tentative voice.

"This place is so grim. Samuel, come home with us. Today."

"No."

"Why?" she whined. "We're your family. We love you and only have your best interests at heart."

"Ha! You cannot claim to love me and have my best interests at heart if you wish me to marry Ebony. A lifetime with her will not make me happy."

"Don't speak to your mother like that," Mr. Gladstone growled.

"I wouldn't have to if she stopped trying to force me down the aisle with that—"

"Don't. Don't call her names. Ebony is a fine girl from an illustrious family."

"If you'd let me finish, you would have simply heard me say 'that girl.'" There was a pause in which one of the men huffed out a breath. "You gave away your motives just now," Samuel went on. "You want me to marry into a good family, not because you or I like Ebony, but because Lord Mellor is a bloody viscount!"

Mrs. Gladstone gave a little sob.

"Don't raise your voice at your mother."

Samuel groaned. "Did you people have to come here *now*?"

"We are not people, Samuel!" his father roared. "We're your parents."

"We care about you," Mrs. Gladstone said in between sniffs. "Please, come home. We won't mention the wedding. Of course, we cannot promise that Ebony won't visit. She will always be welcome in our home."

"Why does she even want to marry me when she can see that I don't want to marry her?"

"She has her heart set on you."

"Don't know why," Mr. Gladstone muttered. "You're a bone-headed fool."

"And that is why I won't be coming home," Samuel said.

"Hush, Henry," Mrs. Gladstone said to her husband.

"I take it Ebony doesn't know about my past, then?" Samuel asked.

Mr. Gladstone grunted. "I made certain of it."

"You've done a very thorough job. There's not been a whiff of scandal in London that I can tell."

"I'm always thorough. It cost me a fortune, but I couldn't have our name muddied by your foolishness."

"My *foolishness*?" There was a long silence before Samuel spoke again. "So you still believe I did it?"

There was no response.

"Mother? Do you no longer think me guilty?"

Sylvia's hand curled around my arm. She tried to tug me away, but I shook my head. I was riveted to the spot and the conversation. I wanted to know Mrs. Gladstone's answer;

not because it would shed any light on what Samuel had done to end up in Newgate, but because he seemed to want to hear her answer so desperately. It was clear from the thin thread of vulnerability running through his voice that he wanted them to believe him innocent. For some reason, so did I.

"Samuel." Mrs. Gladstone sighed. "Samuel, darling, whether you did it or not doesn't matter."

"It does to me!"

"I do know that you won't do it again, and *that's* what's important."

Samuel's chuckle was low, cruel. It sent a shiver down my spine. Sylvia's fingers tightened around my arm. "You think so?" he said. "How can you be sure? Well, Mother? How. Can. You. Be. Sure?"

She gave a little sob.

"Stop this!" Mr. Gladstone said. "Stop this at once. You're frightening your mother."

"That's because I am a frightening creature," Samuel sneered. "My hypnosis has made sure of that."

"No," his father said, equally low and with far more cruelty. "It's because of what you do with it. What you've done."

I pressed my fingers to my lips to stop myself from gasping and giving away our position. Sylvia pressed closer to the door. She no longer tried to force me to leave.

"How did I get to be like this?" Samuel went on. "Hmmm? *Why* can I hypnotize? *What did you do to me?*"

"Nothing!" Mrs. Gladstone cried.

"You must have. Think, Mother. Think back to when I was born, or before. There must be a link between me and… and another hypnotist I know."

"There's another?" Mr. Gladstone asked. "Who?"

"That's none of your affair."

"Another," Mrs. Gladstone said so quietly I almost didn't hear her. "My God."

"It's all right, my dear," Mr. Gladstone said, calmer. "See what you've done, son? You've upset your mother. You always blame others for your mistakes. This hypnotism... you ought to be able to control it by now."

"I can. Mostly," he added softly.

"Please come home," Mrs. Gladstone pleaded. "It's been long enough. You've made your point. We know how angry you are, but it's time to put that behind us. All of it. Come home so we can be a family again."

"No. I like it here. I fit in and the Langleys have been good to me."

"That August Langley is a madman," Mr. Gladstone said. "I asked around about him, after we saw you at Claridge's. He's considered to be a lunatic, fit only for the asylum."

"He's a recluse and a genius. I won't have you disparage him."

"Does it have something to do with that girl?" Mrs. Gladstone asked. "Charity?"

"Leave her out of this."

"I asked around about her too," Mr. Gladstone said. His voice was light, mocking. It filled me with dread. I braced myself.

"Don't, Henry," his wife warned. "It won't help."

"You have quite the spy network, Father," Samuel said, too smoothly. "I suppose you learned that Charity is a teacher at an orphanage."

"We learned much more than that."

"I'm sure you did." His words were benign enough, but the hard, cold edge to Samuel's voice gave away his true feelings.

Whether his father heard it or not, I couldn't be sure. He didn't back away, but kept poking the monster in an attempt to wake it. "Don't you want to know what sort of woman you've been cavorting with, son?"

My stomach rolled. I didn't know why I felt ill listening to the Gladstones discussing me as if I were something they'd scraped off their shoe. Samuel already knew my past, as did

Sylvia, albeit to a lesser extent. Nor should I care what the Gladstones thought of me.

Yet I did.

"She's a whore." Mr. Gladstone's words punched me in the gut, even though I expected them. I wanted to throw up. "It's hardly a secret. She came from the street, where she no doubt whored herself with whoever would pay her a penny."

"Stop it," Samuel hissed.

"Then she raised her petticoats for a better class of gentleman."

"Stop it or so help me I will make you."

"By all means, use her to relieve certain urges," Mr. Gladstone went on.

"Henry!" his wife cried.

"But you must avoid her in any public capacity or the stench of her will stain you—us. I will not allow her to weasel her way into this family."

"Enough!" Samuel exploded. His shout made me jump. My heart was already beating rapidly, but now it wanted to leap out of my chest.

Please don't hit your own father, Samuel.

"It only goes to show how base Langley is if he allows a whore to sit in his drawing room, sipping tea with his guests and his own niece."

Sylvia stiffened and her grip tightened again. I went very still, and waited for Samuel's rage to boil over. It never did. Instead, a vision burst upon me.

That girl was in it again. She sat on the bed, dressed only in her nightshirt, her hands gripping hold of the bedpost as if it would anchor her in a storm. The man whose eyes I looked through was on the bed too. He had hold of her nightshirt at the neck, as if he was about to tear it off. In his other hand he grasped a leather belt with a silver buckle.

Oh God. No. He was going to whip her with it.

CHAPTER 11

The vision must have made the man pause. The girl glanced tentatively over her shoulder at him. At me. Her eyes were red and swollen, and tears streaked down her cheeks. She looked relieved that he'd not torn off her nightgown, but unsure of what to do next.

The vision vanished just as unexpectedly as it had arrived. I was once more back in the corridor at Frakingham. There was silence in the drawing room. Silence everywhere. Yet I could still hear that poor girl's sobs in my head.

I slumped against the wall, shaking. I couldn't stop it. My legs couldn't hold me up and my hands were useless. I crumpled to the floor. Sylvia tried to hold me, but she wasn't strong enough. She knelt alongside me and frowned.

What's wrong? she mouthed.

I shook my head and closed my eyes, but the things I'd seen wouldn't go away. That poor, helpless girl. It was like I was right there in the room with her. No, not with her. Like I *was* her. It could have been me facing the whipping.

Indeed, it *had* been me. I knew it with sickening certainty, that what I saw happening to her had happened to me at the hands of the man known as the master. It was the memory Samuel had blocked. The memory he tried to keep from me.

"You have to go, now," Samuel's steady voice came from the drawing room. Gone was the fierce anger. He sounded exhausted, sad. Had he seen the girl, too?

Unlikely. Usually when I saw through the third person's eyes, Samuel saw through mine. That meant he knew I was listening at the door. He knew I'd heard his father call me a whore.

"But Miss Langley asked us to stay for luncheon," Mrs. Gladstone protested.

"She's withdrawn the offer," Samuel said, heavily. "Go now. I don't want to see you here again."

"We haven't finished our discussion," Mr. Gladstone said. He sounded surprised by the sudden change in his son.

"Don't make me have the footman throw you out. It's so undignified."

Sylvia tugged me up by the arms. *Go!* She mouthed. I allowed her to help me and together we rushed down the corridor. She led me into the music room and sat me down on the piano stool. She stood by the window and announced when the Gladstones' carriage had driven away.

"Good riddance," she said, rejoining me. "What awful people. Especially him." She peered into my eyes. "Are you all right? You look terribly pale and you can't stop shaking. Are you having another turn?"

I looked down at my hands. They were indeed shaking. "I… I received a fright. I'll be all right in a moment."

"That man is a beast. Don't listen to him."

It was ironic that she was now defending my honor when it had seemed to bother her so much when I first arrived. Ah well, perhaps I had judged her incorrectly after all.

"It's not that," I said.

"Samuel!" Sylvia cried.

I looked past her to see Samuel enter. He focused on me so intently I felt like I was the only one in the room, the only thing that mattered. He crouched before me and closed his hand over mine, on my knee. He stroked his thumb over my scars with a tenderness that had my heart aching.

I withdrew my hand. His already troubled eyes clouded further. I couldn't stand to see his turbulence so I looked away.

He stood and took a step backwards. "I'm sorry."

"You have nothing to apologize for," I said. "You cannot control what other people say."

"No, indeed," Sylvia chimed in. "But how do you know that we overheard the conversation?"

"We had a vision," he told her. "I saw through Charity's eyes."

"And I saw through the... that man's." A shudder rippled down my spine. I wanted to tell Samuel about it, but not with Sylvia present. Her world was bright and simple; the only dark spots came when she overheard cruel barbs directed at her guest. I didn't want her to know what the master was doing to that girl.

Samuel crossed his arms over his chest. "I hate my father for what he said. He can rot in hell, as far as I'm concerned."

"Don't say such things," I scolded. "They do care about you, in their own way."

"How can they? They don't know what I want, even when I tell them. Father only wants an heir who will carry on the family name for the next generation."

"Won't your older brother inherit?"

"Yes, but his illness means he's unlikely to marry and have children. Apparently it's up to me, or so my mother says. She hates being the object of gossip, but she certainly likes the idea of her son being married to a viscount's daughter with grand schemes of her own."

Grand schemes? I didn't have the heart to ask him what he meant. I was still so shaken by the vision.

Sylvia plopped down on a chair with a deep sigh. "It's what all parents want for their children. Uncles, too. It's only natural to want your offspring to have the best in life."

"In that case, my parents and I disagree on what the best in life is. They think it's marrying an ambitious viscount's daughter. I think it's sharing a full life with someone I care deeply about."

I didn't dare look at him to see if he was looking at me. I couldn't bear it if he still held a torch for me. "They're your family," I mumbled into my chin. "You should be grateful to have them, and a lovely roof over your head. I assume your father's house is as magnificent as this."

"It depends on your definition of magnificent. It's grander, but it lacks warmth. I'd rather live in a crowded cottage than there with them."

A cottage was better than a derelict house with a leaking roof, furniture made from crates and the threat of the entire thing collapsing in a strong wind.

"Well," Sylvia said, rising. "If you're feeling better, Charity, I must leave you."

"Much better, thank you." I watched her go and waited until she was out of the room before speaking to Samuel. "I saw that girl," I told him. "We have to help her. She's in danger from the master—"

"What sort of danger?"

"He was about to whip her." I swallowed the bile burning my throat.

"Jesus," he muttered. He sat on the chair Sylvia had vacated and rubbed his hand through his hair. "Are you sure?"

I nodded. "I didn't see him to do it, but I'm positive he was going to. She's his prisoner, Samuel. His... plaything."

He squeezed his eyes shut as if he could block out my words, or perhaps my memories. "How can you be certain? She could be his wife."

"Because I know. I know it as clearly as I know that I'm sitting here with you. I feel it. I may not have that memory anymore, but the emotions associated with it have been slowly coming back to me. Fear, anger, horror. When I see her, I *know* what she's going through. It's as if it's happening to me."

He buried his head in his hands, but not before I saw the stricken look in his eyes.

"We *have* to help her, Samuel."

"How? Tell me how we find them and I will, gladly."

That was the problem. Where did we even begin?

***

A telegram arrived the following day from Emily Beaufort. She confirmed that neither she nor Cara had summoned a ghost into a living body, either accidentally or on purpose, and that she knew of no other spirit mediums. She finished with a promise that she would ask.

"Ask who?" Sylvia said, after reading the telegram for the second time. It had been personally delivered by an employee of the Harborough post office, while we ate breakfast. Tommy brought it in to the dining room and read it aloud for us.

"Ghosts," Samuel answered.

Sylvia's lips formed an O.

"Ghosts can come and go from the Waiting Area," he explained. "It's where they accumulate, while they wait to be assigned to their next destination."

"Heaven and hell?"

"I think there are many more categories than those two, but essentially you're right. The final resting place of the deceased, you could say. I would guess that she's going to ask some trusted spirits if another has disappeared unexpectedly."

"How clever. I hope they find one who knows something."

"So do I."

I cornered Samuel after breakfast, out of earshot of Sylvia. She hardly seemed to notice me, anyway. Her owlish gaze followed Tommy as he walked off, pushing a trolley laden with dishes. He had not looked at her or spoken to her since she'd sat down for breakfast. I was glad to see him taking my advice. The last thing I wanted was for Sylvia's heart to be broken over what was a mere diversion for him.

"I can't stop thinking about that girl," I told Samuel. Indeed, I'd lain awake most of the night, wondering what could be done. "We should contact the police in London."

"And tell them what? We have no proof and no idea where to start looking."

"Perhaps if we went to London…" I trailed off. The futility of my own suggestion wasn't lost on me.

"I know this is hard, Charity. It is for me too." I could see the truth of it in his tired, red eyes. "I know you want to help her, but I cannot fathom *how* we can."

He was right. It was a foolish suggestion, but I felt so useless and I despised being useless. I'd rather be dead than sit around all day and sew or play the piano, but it seemed I would have to. I couldn't even return to the school until that man was caught, and how could he be caught when we and the police had so little to go on?

"I'll ride into the village this morning and have the police telegram Scotland Yard about your case. They might have some clues by now."

We both knew that was unlikely. Unless the criminal's description could be matched to a known villain, there was a good chance he would never be caught.

The crunch of wheels on the gravel drive announced a visitor. Samuel opened the door, since neither Tommy nor the maids were nearby. Myer stepped down from an open gig and handed the reins to the stable boy who scampered up to him.

"Good morning," Myer said, tipping his hat to us. "Lovely day."

We exchanged pleasantries as we walked inside. Tommy arrived and took Myer's hat, gloves and coat, then Samuel excused himself and Myer.

"We're expected in Langley's laboratory," he said to me. "Will you be all right, Charity?"

"Had another turn, eh?" Myer asked me. "Must watch those delicate nerves of yours, Miss Evans."

"Thank you for your concern," I said through a false smile.

Samuel looked amused, blast him.

"Tell me, what is it you're doing up there?" I didn't expect a proper answer, as I'd not received one yet, but I thought it worth asking again nevertheless.

"It's complicated," Myer said.

"Perhaps you could try, Samuel, since Mr. Myer is having trouble comprehending it, to explain."

Myer's supercilious smile faltered. "I'm afraid we need to be upstairs. Coming, Gladstone?"

"We've been sworn to secrecy," Samuel told me. "The experiments are still in the early stages and there's a chance they may not work. If I wish to stay at Frakingham, I must abide by Langley's rules and agree to his wishes."

Agree to his wishes? Was Langley only letting him stay if he helped with his experiments? What could those experiments possibly entail?

I watched them climb the staircase, waited a few minutes, then also went up. My footsteps were muffled by the rug covering the floor outside Langley's room, but to me they seemed as loud as the dinner gong.

Listening at Langley's laboratory door proved futile. If they were speaking, I couldn't hear them. Most of the laboratory seemed to be positioned at the far end of the room, away from the door, with the sitting area closer. That proved to be a good thing. I could open the door slightly and peer in without anyone being the wiser.

I turned the doorknob, praying that it didn't squeak. It didn't. I peered through the crack and spotted Samuel and Bollard standing on either side of the large wooden chair with the metal pipes sprouting from it. Myer sat down and the other two proceeded to... dear lord. They were tying him to the chair!

"Good morning, Charity."

I jumped at the sound of Langely's voice and hurriedly shut the door. I spun around, expecting him to be right behind me, but he was further along the corridor. Perhaps he hadn't seen me spying. I hoped.

"Good morning, Mr. Langley. I was just looking for Sylvia. Have you seen her?"

He wheeled himself towards me. "No. She rarely ventures up here. I expect you'll find her downstairs, in the drawing room or music room, or perhaps in the garden. That's where she usually is."

"Yes, of course." I smiled and went to move past him.

Lightning quick, he grabbed my wrist. "Just a moment. I have a question for you."

I swallowed. "Yes?"

"What were you doing just now?"

"I, uh, I was looking for Sylvia."

"Don't lie to me." He didn't snap or growl. His voice was calm and cool. For some reason that made my skin prickle.

"I, I'm sorry."

To my surprise, he let me go. "It's human nature to be curious. I don't blame you. But my work is private, until a time I can publish the final results."

"Are you afraid another scientist will steal your research?"

He seemed startled by my question. "No. The general public would be frightened by what they see in there. They don't understand that the work I do is necessary. The results are important, but an outsider will likely think my methods are... unusual."

"You mean strapping someone to a contraption and hooking those wires and pipes up to him?"

"He will come to no harm."

"Does your work have something to do with Mr. Myer and Samuel's hypnosis?"

"As I told you, my work is private. Now, if you don't mind, I have to go in."

I wanted to ask more questions, but I was acutely aware that my position was a precarious one. I supposed I should be grateful he'd not asked *me* to volunteer to be strapped to the chair.

He began to wheel himself away, but stopped. "You have an inquisitive mind, Charity. You would make a good scientist."

"Thank you. I enjoy working in our little school laboratory. We only teach the rudiments of the sciences to our students, but I've considered taking our studies to a deeper level for the brighter ones."

"Perhaps I can help you there. I'm happy to donate some instruments that I no longer use. Bollard keeps them in the attic for emergencies. It was how I could continue to work, despite the fire destroying most of my lab."

"Thank you. That's very kind and I accept the offer."

Still he did not move away. "I admit to being surprised at your inquisitiveness," he said.

"Oh? Why is that?"

"Isn't it obvious?"

I shrugged. "Not to me."

"You don't seem to want to know anything about the memory you had Samuel wipe."

My body tightened and my insides scrunched into a leaden ball. I didn't know if he expected me to say something, so I remained quiet in the hope that he would stop talking.

He didn't. "Are you not the least bit curious, particularly now, after the attempted kidnap and the visions?"

"No. If I went to such great lengths to block the memory, why would I want it back?"

"Because you're you. You've got a quick, inquisitive mind. I admit to being surprised that you did ask Samuel to remove the memory. You seem like a strong girl." He frowned. "Although, to be fair, that's a more recent development. I can't imagine the quiet girl who came here the first time would have had the gall to sneak around the house, spying into her host's rooms."

Again, I said nothing.

"Am I right, Charity? You *are* braver now?"

"I suppose I am." The truth of it was not lost on me. I had initially hoped that removing the memory would give me a greater capacity to love the children, but it had also lessened my fears. I wasn't afraid of men so much. I didn't avoid the charming ones like I used to. I didn't avoid Samuel.

"Because you no longer have that memory," he went on. "Interesting." His frown turned thoughtful. I got the feeling he was studying me and my answers like he would study a chemical reaction in a test tube.

I shifted my feet and eyed the staircase. Would it be impolite if I just walked away? When I turned back to face him, his gaze had softened and his mouth turned sad. He wheeled himself back to me, a laborious task in the cumbersome chair, and took my hand.

"Bad things happen to good people all the time," he said. "It's the way of the world."

"I know that more than most."

"I suspect you do. Jack has told me much about your lives together and I can only imagine how hard it must have been."

"Hard, yes, but a good life, sometimes, too. We were free and we had one another."

He patted my hand. "I admire your ability to see the good despite the bad. That's why I'm surprised by your cowardly act."

I jerked my hand free. "Cowardly?"

If he regretted his choice of words, he didn't show it. He seemed quite unconcerned about calling someone a coward to their face. "The true measure of a person is how they cope with the bad and how they live their life afterwards. A brave person faces their demons. A coward runs from them."

It took me a moment to catch my breath, but when I did, my temper came with it. "Is that so?" I bent down so that my face was level with his. "Tell me, Mr. Langley, if you were beaten so hard that permanent scars were left on your body, would you want to remember why?"

"Yes," he said, not moving his gaze from mine.

I jerked upright, shocked.

"Because memories serve to teach us," he went on. "Even the bad ones."

"What in God's name do you think I've learned from those beatings?"

"To be afraid; fear taught you caution."

"It restricted me."

"It kept you safe.

"Nonsense. If I'd kept that memory, I would continue to be half a person, a shell only, with my heart hollowed out. I want to love, Mr. Langley. I want to love the children as much as they love me." Hot tears sprang to my eyes, but I would not release them. I was too angry for that. "I could never love them if I'd kept that memory. Never. It was too much, too consuming."

He didn't flinch from my diatribe, didn't look away from my eyes. "Perhaps you didn't give it long enough. I suspect you would have found love again if you wanted it badly enough. Whatever horrible thing happened to you, it did restrict you. I don't deny that. But it's within you to make that restriction temporary, Charity."

"This is nonsense," I spat. "Half-truths, guesses, ifs, buts, maybes. You are not me, Mr. Langley. You do not know what I went through, so do *not* accuse me of cowardice. Good day."

I didn't look back to see if he watched me storm off. I raced down the stairs where he couldn't follow. By the time I reached the bottom, the tears that I'd held back spilled down my cheeks. I couldn't stop them.

I ran out the front door and headed across the lawn to the ruins. When I finally reached them, I plopped down on the grass and leaned back against the base of what once had been a large pillar.

The exercise had tired me, but calmed me too. My tears turned from angry ones to sad ones. Because deep down, I knew Langley was right. I was a coward. And my cowardice had turned Samuel from a charming man into a broken one.

***

I retired to bed early. I had little enthusiasm for the dinner table conversation between Sylvia and Samuel. Samuel must have noticed, because he kept watching me from beneath half-lowered lashes. Sylvia was more interested in discussing an upcoming dinner invitation to the Butterworths' and whether we ought to attend or not. I think I was included in the invitation, but not knowing how long I would be at Frakingham, I thought it best not to reply just yet.

It seemed to take me forever to fall asleep. I couldn't stop thinking about that girl, and Langley's accusation. In the end, I decided I needed to talk to Samuel in the morning. I wanted him to give me back my memory in its entirety. And I wanted to go to London; it was likely that girl was originally from the streets. We could check with the police if any girls had been reported missing, and if not, Tommy and I could tap into our old network of orphans and thieves. There might be rumors floating around. The odds of finding a clue would be long, but it was worth trying.

I had to do something.

Coming up with a plan enabled me to finally fall into a light asleep. Light enough that the click of my door opening had me bolting upright. I reached under my pillow, where I'd stored a knife on my first night. Mrs. Peeble's derringer would have been better, but it was still in the pocket of one of my dresses.

Slowly, slowly, my bedroom door opened wider. My heart hammered in my chest. It was the loudest sound in the room. I tightened my grip on the knife handle and steeled myself. A silhouetted figure entered. A tall, big man.

The same man who'd tried to kidnap me in London.

CHAPTER 12

I wanted to scream and alert the household, but that would only send the attacker scampering away. We needed to catch him. Besides, the nearest room was occupied by Sylvia and I doubted she would be much help in a crisis. It was up to me.

He crept closer to the bed. He seemed so much bigger than last time. Monstrous. How could I ever fight him off on my own?

What if my sweat-slicked palm lost grip on the knife? What if he knew I was awake and was prepared for my attack?

He kept coming. My decision to fight him off alone suddenly seemed pathetic and stupid. So I screamed.

I jumped out of bed at the same moment and kicked, hard. He didn't see my foot coming in the dark and I landed a cringing blow to his groin. He doubled over, wheezing in pain. I lunged and stabbed him in the shoulder.

He reared back and roared. His bear-like paws didn't touch the wound like I'd hoped, but reached for me. I scrabbled backward across the bed and tumbled onto the floor on the other side. I still clutched the knife, but he was prepared for it this time. He may have been injured, but not enough to hinder his movements. He was too strong for me.

"Charity?" came Sylvia's quivering voice at the door.

"Get Tommy and Samuel!" My words were barely out before she was screaming for them.

"Fucking whores!" the attacker shouted. He turned and lumbered towards the door and Sylvia.

"Run!" I yelled at her.

Thank goodness she was as light on her feet as she was loud. She screamed all the way back along the corridor. I heard her door slam shut, followed by the sound of the bolt being driven home. The pounding footsteps of my attacker retreated in the other direction.

I did not chase him.

Samuel was the first to arrive in my room. He skidded to a stop inside my door.

"Charity? Charity, are you all right?"

"Yes." I pressed a hand to my breast in an attempt to slow my heart. It didn't work and it kept trying to hammer its way through my ribs. "That man was here again. The one from London."

He swore and turned to go.

"Stay." My voice was barely a whisper, but he heard me.

He came inside. It was dark, but there was enough light to make out the shape of his face, the shine in his eyes, the stricken downtown of his mouth.

"I won't leave you," he murmured. He gently pried the knife from my fingers and set it down on the mantel. Then he cupped my jaw and rubbed his thumb along my cheek. "I'll be here as long as you want me."

I didn't want a protector—I didn't need one—but his words shattered me. I began to shake and cry. Hot tears poured down my cheeks onto his fingers. His other arm circled me and gently pulled me closer. I rested my head against his shoulder until my tears dried.

Even then I didn't move away. I listened to the thrum of his pulse as it slowed from a wild, arrhythmic beat to a steadier, calmer one. He rested a hand on the back of my neck, under my hair, as if he were holding me in place and didn't want me to move away. I could have, easily, but I didn't want to. I closed my eyes and drew his masculine scent into my lungs.

I don't know how long we stood like that without moving. I heard Tommy arrive and Samuel give him instructions to check the house and secure all doors and windows. Then I once more had his full attention. He didn't try to kiss me or touch me in intimate places. He just held me, as if he knew that was what I needed. I had never been so close to a man without having him attempt to remove my clothing.

It was new, and wonderful.

And then it was too much.

My breathing became heavy again, my chest tight. I broke the embrace and stepped back. His sigh sounded like a protest, but he did not try to stop me.

"Thank you," I said. *Thank you for making me feel safe. Thank you for understanding that I don't want intimacy.* I couldn't tell him either of those things, with the tears still so close, but I hoped he understood it.

"What happened?" he asked.

Tommy and Sylvia entered. She held a large lamp and he had his hand on her back. Bollard came up behind them, blinking in the light.

"The house is secure," Tommy said.

Bollard tapped Sylvia on the shoulder and she jumped. "Don't sneak around, Bollard! Goodness, we've had enough frights for one night."

He bowed an apology, but did not stop frowning.

"It was the same fellow that tried to kidnap me in London," I told them.

Sylvia handed the lamp to Tommy and embraced me. "Are you all right, Charity? Did he hurt you?"

"No. I got a fright, that's all."

"There's blood," Tommy said, looking down at the floor.

"I stabbed him."

"Good." Sylvia patted my arm. "I hope he bleeds to death."

"I don't think he was wounded enough for that."

"We should look for him," Tommy said.

"Not now," Samuel said. "In the morning, when it's light. I don't think we should leave the ladies alone."

Sylvia folded her arms, but it didn't stop her shudder.

"Are you cold?" Tommy sounded concerned. Considering I was the one who'd nearly been kidnapped, I was a little curious as to why he fussed over her. "I'll fetch your shawl."

"I'll come with you," she said. "Then perhaps we should all go to the kitchen and you can make us some chocolate."

It was as good an idea as any. I wasn't going to fall back to sleep and besides, we needed to discuss what to do next.

Bollard slipped away into the darkness, and the rest of us headed downstairs together. Sylvia and I wore our shawls wrapped around our shoulders and the men were dressed in trousers and shirts. Samuel, Sylvia and I sat at the kitchen table as Tommy warmed up the chocolate over the stove. We'd not said a word as we made our way through the quiet house, and now it felt like the silence would smother me.

"He's here," I said, voicing what I suspected everyone was thinking. "The master is nearby."

Sylvia pulled her shawl closed at her throat. "How can you be sure? Perhaps he simply sent his man and he's still in London."

"Perhaps," I murmured. The truth was, I *knew* him to be close yet I couldn't explain how I knew it. I just did.

Tommy gave me the first cup of chocolate. He rested a hand on my shoulder and gently squeezed, reassuring. I smiled up at him as best as I could, but it was difficult to be positive when faced with the worry in his eyes.

He returned to the stove. Samuel traced a knot in the wood on the table surface, his gaze intent on his task. Sylvia's focus switched to Tommy then back to me. She pressed her lips together and also looked down at the table.

Tommy, oblivious, set a cup of chocolate in front of each of them then fetched his own and joined us. I wanted to tell Sylvia and Samuel that nothing untoward was happening between Tommy and me, but I didn't. There were more important events to discuss, and I was a little miffed that it should enter their heads at all. I may not have been too discriminate with my bedfellows in the past, but I didn't have an affair with *every* man I met.

Thinking of men in *that* way had me once again focusing on the master and the girl. My head ached and I thought for a moment I would experience a vision, but I didn't. I did, however, remember.

Not all of it, just pieces. The sharp sting of the belt across my back and the ache of the wound afterwards. The desperate scrabble at the door in an attempt to escape. The thrashing I received from the master's brute after almost succeeding in getting out through the window, one time.

I concentrated hard on exploring the broken memories, but could only manage an objective view of the pieces, as an outsider would see them. A deeper exploration eluded me. I didn't *want* to remember everything, yet I needed to. As Langley had said, fear kept us safe, and fear was borne from our memories. Without remembering, I would never be safe from the master again.

Nor could I fully move forward.

"We cannot be sure where he is," Samuel said. "Until we are, we must assume that he's here. We know his man is. Charity must be protected from him."

"Sylvia, too," Tommy said. On her gasp, he added, "We don't know if he'll take anyone in Charity's place or not. I'd rather be safe than sorry."

"As would I," I said.

"The question is," Samuel added, "how did he know where to find you?"

"Could someone from the school have told him?" Sylvia asked.

Tommy grunted. "If they did, I'll be sure to have words with them when next I'm in London."

"No one knew where to find me," I said. "Mrs. Peeble knew I was going to a friend's house in Hertfordshire, but not the name or exact location."

"Then who else?" Sylvia asked.

Samuel's fingers whitened around his cup. "Myer."

I shrugged. "How could he? He doesn't know the man."

"So he says."

"You don't believe him?" It was so sinister, so horrible, that I didn't want to believe him. How could Myer lie about such a thing? He was slippery, but not monstrous. Was he?

"His motives are certainly not pure. I think he would do almost anything to gain information on the supernatural world. If the master went to him and asked how to find you in exchange for knowledge, I have no doubt that Myer would tell him about me and my link to Frakingham."

"How would the master know that you two are acquainted with Myer?" Sylvia asked.

"Perhaps it was a stroke of luck," I whispered. Oh lord. I saw the connections now. "It would be natural to ask the head of the Society for Supernatural Activity about the visions he was suddenly experiencing. Myer may have told him about ours, and how to find me, in exchange for information." As a ghost in possession of a living body, the master would have access to the Waiting Area, other spirits and supernatural information not privy to us. A gold mine, for someone like Myer.

"I detest that man," Sylvia spat. Her vehemence quickly vanished with another shudder of her thin shoulders.

"It's almost daylight," Samuel said, nodding at the window. "We'll pay Myer a visit at the Butterworths' immediately after breakfast."

"That's a little early," Sylvia said.

"I don't care if I have to drag him out of bed myself. He's going to bloody well answer us properly, this time."

"And if he doesn't?" I asked.

He said nothing. He didn't need to. We all understood what he'd do. It was written into every groove around his pursed lips and every wretched shadow in his eyes. He would hurt him.

***

I cornered Samuel alone at the coach as we waited for Sylvia, but he spoke before I had a chance to say anything.

"Are you all right?" he asked, his gaze flicking over me. "Any ill effects?"

"Some, but none that can be seen."

He frowned and half shook his head in question.

"The memory block isn't working anymore."

The muscle in his jaw corded, but he made no other movement. "You've remembered everything?"

"Not quite everything. Only a few actual memories and some... instincts I suppose you'd call them."

He blew out a breath and his eyes briefly fluttered closed. "Good."

"I want to remember all of it."

"Why? It won't help you identify him."

"I know. But I *need* to know the rest of it, Samuel."

"You don't. I assure you, it's best if you don't remember."

I sighed. I suspected this would be a difficult task. "I don't expect you to fully understand, but please, just give me my memories back."

"No."

"Samuel, they're my memories and I want them unblocked."

"No. It's a bad idea."

"It's not working, anyway."

He looked skyward. "Charity," he said heavily, "you don't yet recall everything and I think that's as it should be."

I crossed my arms. "You're bloody stubborn."

"I only have your best interests at heart."

Tommy escorted Sylvia down the steps of the house. I watched them, but spoke to Samuel through my clenched jaw. "I assure you I'm capable of being mistress of my own life as well as my own memories."

"If that were the case, why did you have me block them in the first place?"

I didn't say anything. There was no answer that didn't make me feel like a coward, running from my fears instead of facing them.

"Why do you want them back, anyway?" he asked quietly so the others couldn't hear.

"Because you're troubled by them and a problem shared is a problem halved, as the proverb says."

"Perhaps," he said. "But I won't be sharing that problem with you."

***

The Butterworths' house wasn't a manor house on the scale of Frakingham, but it was a pretty place nevertheless, with pitched roofs and gabled windows. Situated on a rise at one end of Harborough, it had a magnificent vista over countryside, village and babbling stream. A curtain fluttered in one of the windows on the top floor, but I couldn't see anyone.

"Little Jane up to her tricks again," Samuel said, following my gaze. He, Sylvia and I had driven to the village in the Langley coach. Tommy rode beside the driver. He wouldn't allow us to go without him.

"Who's Jane?" I asked.

"The youngest Butterworth girl. She's quite the brave little thing."

"She has a head for mysteries and adventures," Sylvia said with a disapproving scowl. "Quite the handful, I would think."

"What are the names of the twins again?" I asked. They'd told me all about them, but I'd already forgotten. My mind kept wandering to other things. Darker things.

"Julia and Jennifer," Sylvia said. "I do hope they're not home. They're such silly creatures."

Samuel flashed me a tired smirk. Clearly he thought the same as me—how silly must the girls be if *Sylvia* disparaged them?

Our arrival seemed to throw the household into turmoil. It was definitely too early for callers. Although Mrs. Butterworth was having breakfast, her husband and daughters were not up yet, it would seem.

"My apologies," she said as she bustled into the drawing room where we waited. Indeed, we'd waited for almost fifteen minutes before she arrived, which made me think she hadn't actually been at breakfast but still abed. Her hair appeared to be hastily arranged too and the ribbons of her cap weren't yet tied up under her chin. "Such lazy creatures."

"We do apologize for our early visit," Sylvia said. "We wouldn't have come if it wasn't vitally important to speak to your guest, Mr. Myer."

"Hmmm?" Mrs. Butterworth hardly seemed to hear her. She was staring at me. Sylvia apologized again and introduced us. "My goodness," Mrs. Butterworth murmured. "Aren't you a pretty creature? Quite something extraordinary."

I felt my face heat. I was used to people thinking me pretty, but it certainly didn't get easier to hear, even when their comments were kind. Whether hers were meant as a kindness or not, I couldn't be sure.

Samuel cleared his throat. "Is Mr. Myer here this morning?"

"Hmmm? Oh yes, Everett." Her cheeks colored and she touched a hand to the hair curling out from beneath the cap. She looked very much like a debutante in love. I hadn't quite accepted the fact that she was having a liaison with Myer, but it seemed that I'd been wrong. I suddenly felt ill at ease. Although I was no innocent when it came to the tangled relationships between men and women, I drew the line at adultery.

"His valet is attending him now. He'll be down shortly."

Indeed, he arrived almost as soon as she'd finished speaking. He bowed to us, smiling. He didn't look in the least concerned about the early hour. He was impeccably dressed as usual, but his whiskers were a little wayward when ordinarily they were smoothed down with wax.

"You wished to see me?" he asked.

"Did you tell that man where to find Charity?" Samuel said with a quietly ominous tone.

Myer frowned. "Who?"

"The third person sharing our visions."

Mrs. Butterworth gasped. "Visions?"

"Perhaps you could see to bringing us some tea, Mrs. Butterworth," Myer said to her.

"Yes," she muttered. "I think we require tea." Instead of tugging on the bell pull, she left the drawing room altogether.

"Don't mind her," Myer said, watching her go. "I can erase this meeting from her memory."

Samuel stepped up to him and gripped Myer's vest at his chest. Myer flinched. "Don't use your hypnosis on innocents unless they ask for it. Understand?"

"Calm down, Gladstone. I would think you have suitably impressed the ladies with your bravado by now."

"Let him go, Samuel," I said quietly. "We want to talk to him, not start a brawl."

Samuel obeyed and stepped back, but did not take his fierce gaze off Myer.

"Well?" I prompted. "Did you tell anyone about my link to Frakingham?"

Myer tugged on his vest to iron out the creases. "I most certainly did not. I don't know who the fellow is, and even if I did, I would have no reason to divulge your whereabouts. What makes you think I did it?"

"He sent his man after me last night."

Myer swore under his breath. "Thank goodness you're all right."

"I received nothing more than a fright. But the thing is, he now knows where to find me. How could he have possibly done that if he doesn't know where I am?"

"Surely someone from the school told him."

"None knew where I went."

Myer stroked his side whiskers in thought. "A vision, perhaps? Could he have seen Frakingham through your eyes and recognized it? Or someone spoke of the house while you were under the influence of a vision?"

Samuel and I exchanged glances. "Yesterday, when you met with your parents," I said. "If you saw through my eyes then he probably saw through yours. Did either of your parents happen to mention where they were at that particular moment?"

He shrugged. "I can't recall. Although I can see what you're seeing, I cannot hear. Besides, I was preoccupied with being inside your eyes, so to speak."

"Oh my God." Sylvia flounced onto the sofa. She stared at me, her mouth ajar. "Mr. Gladstone did indeed give away a clue. He said something like, 'They call this place Freak House! You must be as mad as Langley himself to want to live here.'"

"That would be enough," Myer said. "Freak House is rather a well-known name for Frakingham, among certain circles."

Sylvia sighed. "Here, too."

Samuel sat beside her and groaned.

"At least we know, now," I said. "Our apologies, Mr. Myer. We shouldn't have accused you like that."

"I understand." He gave us a tight smile. "Now, is there anything else? I'm rather famished and my breakfast awaits."

"Thank you, no. We'll be on our way."

"Did you contact the Beauforts?" he asked as we headed out. There was no one about in the entrance hall, not even a footman or maid. Mrs. Butterworth had not returned either, with or without tea. I wondered how much she knew about the paranormal, or if she knew anything at all. She must have

174

been aware of Myer's interest. Perhaps she was keeping the servants away so they wouldn't overhear our strange conversation. Nevertheless, we kept our voices low.

"We sent a telegram," Samuel said. "They know of no other mediums, but will ask about any known possessions."

"Good, good."

"We'll send another telegram today," Samuel said, more to me than anyone else. "They need to come out here and help remove the master's spirit."

I nodded. I felt some comfort at the thought of having the Beauforts join us. They were a knowledgeable family when it came to the supernatural. I felt my own lack of information keenly.

"Indeed," Myer intoned. "They'll know an incantation to oust the ghost."

He opened the door for us. Sylvia and I exited, but Samuel did not. "What happens if the body the ghost is possessing is rendered useless?" he asked Myer. "Say he's knocked unconscious or dies?"

Sylvia's gulp was audible. "I think I need air." She pressed her fingers to her temple then stepped down to the drive and joined Tommy at the coach.

"The ghost could jump from its host into a nearby body, but he must do it in the moment between consciousness and sleep, or death. Otherwise he would be trapped inside the host until either the body recovers or the medium summons the spirit out."

Samuel nodded. "Good to know."

"If you plan on knocking him out, then I advise you to move away very quickly or the spirit will end up possessing you."

It was an interesting idea, and one that could work if we got caught without a medium. Even if the Beauforts raced out of London, it would take them much of the day to reach us by train; longer, by coach. "Thank you, Mr. Myer," I said. "You've been a great help.

Samuel put out his arm to escort me down the steps, but I shook my head. "If you don't mind, I have a question I'd like to ask Mr. Myer in private."

He blinked at me. I thought he was going to ask me what it was, but then he gave a perfunctory bow and headed down the steps alone. He did not join Sylvia in the cabin, but waited with Tommy. Although he wasn't looking directly at me, I suspected he was watching me out of the corner of his eye.

"What can I do for you, Miss Evans?"

"I would like to know if you can remove the memory block Samuel placed on me."

"Ah. No, I can't. He placed it, so only he can remove it."

"He's refusing to."

"Then you must ask again and again until he does. It is your memory, after all. He has no right to keep it from you if you want it back."

"I think I made a mistake in asking him to block it. I thought it would make everything better, make *me* better, but..." I shrugged, unsure how much I wanted to tell this man.

"But now you feel incomplete without it."

It was as if he saw right into me and knew what I was thinking. "I've been recalling things, lately. Sometimes it's only a feeling, other times it's actually pieces of the puzzle. It happens whenever I experience a vision or at extreme moments. Last night, during the attempted kidnap, for example."

His whiskers twitched as he moved his mouth from side to side in thought. "I have a suggestion for you," he finally said. "It won't be an easy thing to do, but it might help you remember everything if Gladstone continues to refuse."

"What is it?"

"If pieces of your memory are slotting into place whenever you experience a vision or turmoil related to that man, then you should experience them more often. Please, hear me out before you protest." He glanced past me to

Samuel, now openly watching us, his arms crossed over his chest. "I suggest you immerse yourself in the quest to find the man."

"I will do that anyway."

"Yes, but be an active participant, not a bystander. You must experience the emotions that have so far triggered the return of the memory pieces. Do you know which emotion has the most influence?"

"Fear," I whispered.

"Then my suggestion is that you experience fear. It won't be easy, as I said."

"No." I looked to Samuel. He glared back. "Nor do I think putting myself in danger will be a good idea. I don't want to worry anyone." Indeed, it was an odd suggestion for a gentleman to make of a young woman, knowing the circumstances. I couldn't imagine Jack, Samuel or any man of my acquaintance advising me to put myself at risk.

"Ah, well," Myer said. "It's up to you to decide if the cost is worth the outcome. Perhaps you're right and you should wait for Gladstone to give you the memory back. Given time, I'm sure he'll understand."

I thanked him and joined Samuel at the coach. He held the door open for me then followed me into the cabin. Tommy folded up the step then climbed onto the driver's seat.

"All three girls are there, now," Sylvia said, peering out the window and up to the top floor of the house. "How curious. I wonder why they didn't come and say hello."

"I think their mother may not have liked our conversation," I told her. "It's not something young girls should hear."

"It's not something anyone should hear. It's bad enough that Mrs. Butterworth is aware of your visions, but I am glad she didn't hear our talk of possession. She already thinks us all mad."

I tried to catch Samuel's attention, but he did not look at me.

Our journey was a short one. We stopped at the post office, where Samuel went inside to send another telegram to the Beauforts, requesting their company to help us in our ghostly matter.

"I do so wish to see Mrs. Beaufort again," Sylvia said on a sigh as he rejoined us. "A pity the circumstances aren't friendlier. Do you think Miss Moreau will come with them?"

"I hope so," I said, hardly listening. Samuel would still not look at me.

It wasn't until we arrived back at Frakingham that he gave me his attention. He helped Sylvia down from the coach and then me. Our gloved hands touched. He did not immediately let go.

"I asked Myer if he could remove my memory block," I said, once Sylvia was out of earshot.

The coach rumbled away and Tommy left us alone. Samuel sighed. He seemed suddenly deflated, as if he'd decided to let go of the very thing propping him up. "I suspected as much."

"He couldn't do it."

He inclined his head. "Are you disappointed?"

"Somewhat. Samuel, will you reconsider?"

He shook his head. "Please don't ask again. I find it rather tortuous, refusing you anything." His impish smile was reminiscent of the carefree Samuel of old, the one not weighed down by my memories.

"I wouldn't ask if it wasn't important to me."

He closed his eyes and sucked in his breath. "Charity… don't let this come between us. I cannot give it back to you. I can't do that to you."

My temper rose, heating my skin, but I kept it from showing. He was trying to protect me and I couldn't fault him on that score. It irked me that I wasn't mistress of my own past, something I'd not expected to feel when I initially asked him to block it, yet it was solely my doing, not his.

I blew out a breath and my frustration with it. "It won't come between us." I took his arm and gave him a smile that had him blushing to his ears in the most endearing way.

Ordinarily his reaction would have me retreating inside myself, but I resisted the urge to pull back. My old fears may be resurfacing in small ways, but I would not let them conquer me.

We walked back into the house together. It was pleasant and I didn't want to sour the moment by telling him what Myer had said I should do to remove the block. Besides, I didn't want Samuel suspecting what I was up to.

CHAPTER 13

Samuel ordered all the doors and windows to be locked. Nobody was allowed out for a walk, so it was a blessing that it rained for most of the day. I couldn't concentrate on even the simplest tasks. Not even Langley's extensive library offered any comfort. I was sitting in one of the large leather armchairs, re-reading the same page of a Thomas Hardy novel for the hundredth time when Tommy came to fetch me in the afternoon.

"Mr. Butterworth is here," he said.

"He wants to see me?"

"All of you. He wants to apologize for not being at home this morning to greet you. 'Not being at home' is toff-speak for 'I was too bloody lazy to get out of bed.'"

I giggled. "I know what it means. I've lived with toffs before, remember?"

His grin faded. He looked down at his feet. Tommy never liked being reminded of who and what I'd been before I became a teacher. He must also be feeling the pressure of our situation enormously, too. He and Samuel were the only young, able-bodied men in the household, although Bollard looked quite strong, if not youthful.

"Charity, be careful." He spoke as if he could will me to stay out of trouble.

I lay my hand on his arm. "Of course."

"I wish Jack was here."

"So do I. But Samuel has been marvelous, as have you."

"Samuel isn't Jack. Neither am I."

"We cannot always rely on him to help us get out of scrapes. It's good for me, knowing he can't come to my rescue."

"I s'pose."

"Stop worrying. I will be alert, as ever. Now we know what we're up against, all will be well. The Beauforts will be here soon, anyway."

"By late afternoon is my guess," he said.

"Very well, Dawson," I said in my most upper-class accent. "Lead the way to Mr. Butterworth."

We found him in the drawing room with Samuel. Sylvia was nowhere to be seen. The Harborough mayor was a short man, shorter than his wife who was about my height, but it gave him a jolliness that I suspected was important for a mayor, if he wanted to be re-elected.

"Ah, yes," Mr. Butterworth said, extending his hand to me. "My wife said you were a beauty and she was spot on."

I accepted his praise and dared not look at Samuel, lest the blush I was trying to hold back escaped. "I'm sorry we missed you this morning," I said.

He apologized for his absence. "Urgent mayoral business to attend to. I was out and about early." The doughy skin around his eyes folded as he smiled. He had a lumpy face, like a child's attempt at molding a clay figure.

"It was good of you to come all this way just to apologize," I said.

"Oh, I didn't. Well, not exactly. I was just telling Mr. Gladstone about someone new to the village that may be of interest to him, and you too."

I turned my unblinking gaze on Samuel. He leaned forward, intent on Butterworth.

"Mr. Myer took it upon himself to ask me about any newcomers to the village after you left this morning. He said he was inquiring on your behalf, although he wouldn't tell me what it was about."

My heart leapt into my throat. Myer didn't know all the details of what the master meant to me, nor would he, but I still didn't like the idea of him discussing what he did know with others. Butterworth was clearly waiting for an explanation. He would get none.

"And?" Samuel prompted. "Are there any?"

"Yes, as a matter of fact. A gentleman arrived yesterday. He rented rooms off Mrs. Turner in the village."

"Did he have someone with him?" I asked. "What did he look like? What's he doing here?"

Butterworth held up his hands and chuckled. "Slow down, Miss Evans. I believe he had a valet with him. They arrived by train in the late afternoon. As to what he looks like, or why he's here, I don't know, I haven't met him."

"Where does this Mrs. Turner live?" Samuel asked.

"In the large, neat place on the corner of Beckett and Crown Streets. You can't miss it."

Samuel stood before Butterworth had even finished his sentence. He headed for the door, but seemed to collect himself and stopped. "Forgive me, Mr. Butterworth. Charity will see you out. I have to go."

"Wait!" I cried. "Do you think it wise to go now, without making a plan first?"

"We must strike immediately. I'll take Tommy and come up with a plan on the way." He took my hand. "Don't be afraid, Charity. Stay here, keep the doors locked." He nodded at a gawping Butterworth and left.

"What, pray, is going on?" Mr. Butterworth said. "Who is the fellow at Mrs. Turner's?"

"A man who may or may not have tried to abduct me."

"Bloody hell," he muttered into the folds of his chins. "There is never a dull moment at Frakingham."

"Indeed not. Can I offer you tea, Mr. Butterworth?" It was the polite thing to do, but I just wanted him to leave. I needed to take up a position in the tower room and watch for Samuel's and Tommy's return. My nerves would be wrecked until they came home.

"Tea would be very welcome," he said.

I tugged on the bell pull and a maid arrived shortly after. I asked her to bring tea and to find Sylvia.

Mr. Butterworth prattled on about mayoral affairs. I hardly heard him. My mind was occupied with other things, not the least of them listening for sounds of Samuel and Tommy's departure. It seemed like an age, but eventually the pounding of hooves on the drive announced they'd left.

Sylvia arrived at the same time as the tea. The maid deposited the tray and left. Sylvia handed a cup to Mr. Butterworth, but he set it down immediately and came to me. He grabbed my hand between both of his own.

"If I can be of any assistance to you, dear Charity, please come to me." He wasn't quite kneeling in front of me, but he did bend awkwardly over me, like a man in pain.

I tried to withdraw my hand, but he didn't let it go. He smiled and it wasn't the smile of a friendly, jolly fellow, but an earnest one. His eyes dilated as he stared into mine with an intensity that sent a violent shiver down my spine. His behavior was odd.

I tried to remove my hand again. The more I pulled, the firmer his grip became and the harder his eyes. They were gleaming now, like two small polished stones. I peered into them and didn't see a friendly man. I saw a monster.

Inside the body of the mayor was the master. My tormentor.

My hand stilled. My heart ground to a halt. I stopped trying to get away. Stopped breathing. Fear swamped me, insidious and paralyzing. It brought back the memories. They slammed into me, thick and fast. I remembered how pathetic and small the master used to make me feel, how helpless. I'd cried through the beatings, and when he pressed the end of his burning cigar to my raw flesh, I'd cried more. Yet I'd accepted the cruelty, because there was no means of escape. Not until Jack had rescued me. Not until the master had died, his flesh turned to ashes.

Yet here he was again, inside the body of a man trusted by Samuel and Sylvia. I couldn't think how that had happened. My brain was being smothered by fear as surely as a damp blanket smothers a flame.

Sylvia's voice broke through the fog. "This is pleasant," she said cheerfully. "We don't get many visitors."

Butterworth's smile stretched his lips thin. "Most pleasant."

Their voices lifted the fog somewhat, allowing me to think a little. I needed to escape, yes, but most of all, I had to get Sylvia to safety.

I didn't try to remove my hand from Butterworth's. Instead, I returned his smile. It took enormous effort. "Sylvia, would you mind very much asking the maid to bring us something to eat."

"She did," she said. "Cream puffs. Try some, Mr. Butterworth."

"Perhaps something else," I said without taking my gaze off his. Nor did he look away from me. It was like we were locked in a silent battle of wills. A battle I knew I'd lose.

"But these are delicious!" Sylvia cried.

"Just do it!"

She fell silent. My outburst probably confused her, perhaps hurt her feelings, too. It didn't matter. All that mattered was getting her out of the room to safety.

"Please," I added. "I don't like cream puffs."

"Well," she huffed. "I'm sure we can find something else for your highness to nibble on. Excuse me, Mr. Butterworth." She went to the bell pull.

I was about to ask her to go down to the kitchen in person when Mr. Butterworth suddenly let go of my hand. He leapt up, and in a movement so swift as to be unnatural for someone with his stocky frame, he grasped a statuette off the table and hit Sylvia over the head with it.

She crumpled to the floor without a sound.

I bit back my scream, but the fear rose again, fiercer than before. I couldn't stop shaking. Butterworth took hold of my hand and jerked me to my feet so hard my shoulder screamed in pain.

"Do not make a sound," he growled. "Or you'll be coming with me to the afterlife faster than you can blink."

I didn't need the threat to keep me silent. The fear did that. It paralyzed my tongue and numbed my head all over again.

He dragged me out of the house, to the coach waiting near the front steps. He shoved me roughly in the back so that I fell onto the cabin floor. I tried to stand, but he pressed his boot against my knee.

I gasped in pain and he removed his boot. I remained where I was as he pulled the cabin door closed. The driver urged the horses forward with a crack of his whip and the coach raced off. No one shouted for us to stop. No one followed us. No one even knew we'd left and that Sylvia lay unconscious on the floor in the drawing room. Samuel and Tommy were in the village, looking for a ghost. A ghost who was now taking me away to plunge me into a nightmare all over again.

But this time I would not let the nightmare become real. I was a different woman, now. I was no longer a child desperate to escape the streets, desperate to be loved. I had much to live for: the orphans, my friends, a fulfilling life. And that other girl, the one I'd seen in my visions, needed me. I could be brave, for her. I *would* be brave.

If only my newfound resolve would tell my brain that. The fear had me curling into a ball as far away from his feet as possible and shaking as if it were the depths of winter. The fear could cripple me if I let it. The more afraid and useless I became, the easier I would succumb to the master's sadistic wishes.

Only the weight of the contents of my pocket lent me enough strength to keep me alert.

The master's bleak, soulless eyes settled on me, pinning me to the floor as thoroughly as his boot had done. Butterworth had a soft face, but somehow the master's spirit made the bloated skin seem harder. He'd been a tall, imposing man when he was alive. I remembered that; the sharp blade of his cheekbones, the nip of his teeth when he kissed me, the power in his long fingers. He wouldn't like being inside a body like Butterworth's. I wondered why he'd chosen it, but then I stopped wondering anything when he kicked me in the shin.

"That got your attention." He chuckled. "I can't believe I've finally got you, after all these years."

"You... you've been looking for me?"

He snorted. "Don't flatter yourself, Charity. And did I give you permission to speak? No, I don't believe I did. Remind me to whip you for it when I get you home."

Home. Where was that? Nearby? London?

Suddenly the task ahead seemed overwhelming. How could I escape this man? I couldn't last time, not on my own. I'd needed Jack's help. Jack was far away, now. Samuel and Tommy might as well be, too. We'd not known where to find the master before, and they were still in the dark. They would return to Frakingham after discovering Mrs. Turner's boarder dazed and unable to account for the last few months, or even years, of his life. They would find Sylvia unconscious and learn that Butterworth took me. But the master was too clever to take me back to the mayor's house.

I wanted to ask him where we were going, but my voice wouldn't work. It was as frozen as the rest of me. So I waited and bided my time until we fetched that other girl. *If* he planned on fetching her. Perhaps he had already let her go, knowing he would soon have me. Perhaps he'd killed her.

The coach raced on, not slowing down for bumps or ditches. The rough ride finally came to an end after perhaps thirty minutes.

"Don't say a word when you get out," he said, "or I'll not only kill you, but I'll kill the other girl, too."

I swallowed heavily and fixed him with as stern a glare as I dared.

"You may speak," he said.

"Who is she?" I ventured.

"Just another whore like you."

I flinched. I'd been called that many times, most recently by Samuel's parents, but never had it made me feel as filthy as a sewer.

"You can't escape that term, can you? Whore." He chuckled. "You can't escape me, either. You must have thought you were free, after I died. How you would have rejoiced! Ah, but you see, you and I are bound in this life and the next. We belong together, Charity. For eternity."

The cabin door opened, revealing the same thick-set man who'd tried to kidnap me in London, and again last night. Smith, his name was. I remembered it now. Just Smith. He grinned and held out his hand for me to take. I did and stepped down from the cabin as if I were a lady heading off to a ball.

We were alone at a building site, surrounded by trees. There were no workers, no passersby, and no hope that anyone would stumble across us. The site was isolated, the only access being the road on which we'd just driven. It led back through a dense woodland to goodness knew where.

Butterworth—the master—breathed in deeply. "Such a peaceful place. Can you hear birds, Charity? And the breeze rustling the leaves? So serene. A perfect place to die."

I focused on my surroundings and not his voice or words. I took it all in. The building itself was half finished and would be impressive, once complete. The timber frame stretched three stories high, but the brick walls only covered the lower floor. Tools lay abandoned alongside planks of wood and piles of bricks. I wanted to ask him what purpose the building would have when it was finished, but he hadn't given me permission to speak again. I knew from past experience that asking questions could lead to a painful lesson in obedience.

"Come and meet your playmate," the master said. "She's waiting for you."

I took the arm he offered and we picked our way through the building site. Smith tethered the horses and followed closely behind. If an outsider stumbled upon us, we would have appeared normal, like a regular couple inspecting their building's progress. Yet, if the imaginary outsiders looked at my face, they would have seen the naked fear in my pale skin and round eyes.

We headed into the building itself and made our way through several rooms until we reached some smaller ones at one end of the structure. Smith opened a trapdoor in the wooden floor and indicated I should climb down first. "After you, Miss Charity. You're not afraid of the dark anymore, are you?"

I was terrified. He knew that. He and the master used to leave me in a darkened room, naked and cold, until I began to go mad, wondering what they planned for me upon my release.

I descended the ladder, forcing myself to put one foot ahead of the next. *Keep going, Charity. Swallow the fear.* Easier said than done.

A rustle below set my nerves jumping. I stopped and peered down, but it was as dark as a well. I couldn't even make out shadows. Smith, descending after me, didn't stop. He stepped on my hand.

I screamed as pain ripped through my fingers and up my arm. Mercifully, he lifted his foot. I withdrew my hand and cradled it against my breast.

"You've become soft, Charity," came the master's amused voice from above. "You never used to cry out so loud. Well, perhaps in the beginning. You've forgotten everything you learned."

My face crumpled. Hot tears stung my eyes. I let them fall, here in the dark where they couldn't be seen. How had I reached this point all over again? Despite my resolve to not let him win, not to succumb to the numbing fear, I felt myself slipping into an abyss of darkness, similar to the actual one I was stepping into.

"Move!" Smith snarled.

I used my injured hand as best as I could to steady myself as I descended. I stepped onto the floor and inched away from the ladder. I didn't dare reach out and feel my way around. It would be just like the master to hide traps in the dark. I tucked my injured hand against my chest. The pain had dulled somewhat, to a steady, hot throb. Hopefully there were no broken bones. I would be needing it.

Smith struck a light and lit a lamp. He hung it from a low beam. The lamp's glow illuminated the bulging features of Smith himself and Butterworth's softer ones. Its light didn't quite reach the corners of what appeared to be a large basement. I shivered, partly from the cold, but mostly because I felt as if I were being buried alive. The thick walls were too close, the ceiling too low. Despite the drop in temperature from being underground, sweat beaded on my brow and turned my palms slick.

A sniff came from the shadows off to my right. My heart leapt into my throat and I took an involuntary step closer to the master. His throaty chuckle had me taking a step back in the other direction.

"It's only Wendy," he said. "Come out, Wendy. Meet your predecessor."

A figure emerged from the shadows. It was her, the girl from my visions. She was alive. Relief made me forget myself. I ran to her, but she shrank away and ducked her head, as if she expected a slap.

"I won't harm you," I whispered. "I'm going to help."

Her gaze flicked past me. I turned just in time to receive a blow from Smith's hand across my face. The force of it sent me careening into the wall. Searing pain sliced through my injured hand again as I put it out to break my fall.

"I didn't give you permission to speak," the master roared. "Do you not remember, Charity? Hmmm? You need my permission to speak, to sing, to go, to stay, for everything!"

I whimpered, then grew annoyed at how pathetic it made me sound. If I was to get out of this, I needed to be strong. Strong and clever. And I *would* get out. Not just for me, but for the girl, too. I *had* to, if I wanted to live. The master was dead, and he wanted me to join him.

We belong together. For eternity.

I wasn't ready to leave this world. I wanted to live. Merely acknowledging that fortified me beyond measure. Years ago, the last time I'd been in the master's clutches, I'd not been so determined. I'd not had as much to live for as now.

I eyed the girl again. She was tall and willowy, like me. She couldn't have been more than about seventeen. Her long blonde hair looked clean, if not well styled, and her clothes were new and pretty. The master liked his girl to be nicely presented. I remembered that, too. Remembered so much, now. Samuel's memory block had completely worn off.

Samuel. He and Tommy would have returned to the house from the village. They would be frantic with worry.

I shoved thoughts of them aside. I needed to concentrate on my situation and assume I wouldn't be rescued. It was up to me.

The master came up to us. He was a little shorter than me, in Butterworth's form, reaching only to my nose. He rested a hand on my hip. So gentle. That's how he'd sucked me into his sinister world in the first place, with tenderness, sweet words and handsome looks. He'd been the perfect gentleman, utterly charming, until he'd drawn me into his lair. Then he locked the door, shed the charming facade, and transformed into a monster.

"Wendy has been keeping me company while I waited for you." His breath brushed my neck, warm and putrid. "She's not as beautiful as you, of course. Her essence is a little lackluster, shall we say. You, Charity, are as beautiful inside as you are out. That's what I've always loved about you. It's what I've always wanted."

I didn't dare speak or move; he hadn't given me permission. The only part of me that felt alive was my pounding heart, its beat fierce as it drummed out an erratic rhythm that echoed through my body.

"I had hoped to find you one day, Charity, but I never dreamed it could happen. Those visions were a stroke of luck, were they not?" He nuzzled into my neck. His tongue slithered across my skin above my collar. My insides recoiled, but I remained still on the outside. "I'm curious. Why do they happen?"

"I don't know," I said. "I was hypnotized and, ever since, we've been having visions."

"The hypnotist is the other fellow I met today, eh? Handsome devil. I'd wager you and he have enjoyed each other's beauty on more than one occasion." He nibbled my ear. I endured it without pulling away, just. "Tell me, does he need to hypnotize you to get you to do what he wants, or do you spread your legs for him willingly? Like you did for me."

I never did it willingly for you. That's what I wanted to tell him. I wanted to spit on him, kick him, hurt him. But I did not.

My gaze slipped to Wendy. She watched us, her expression wary. She kept her back to the wall, which meant she'd learned to keep her enemies in view. Good. She was cleverer than she looked.

The master let me go long enough to grab my hair. He pulled it, forcing me to bend backwards so that my face was beneath his.

"How would you like to die, Charity?" he murmured.

Wendy began to cry. I wanted to tell her to be quiet, so as not to attract attention to herself, but I didn't want the master or Smith to hit me again. I needed my wits about me.

"I don't want to die," I told him, my voice quivering.

He chuckled and let me go. "That's too bad, because it's already been decided. I've waited and waited and now I finally get to rest with you in my arms. So, what will it be? I could cut your throat, have Smith beat you to death, or strangle you."

"Strangle," I said quickly.

"Very well." He let me go and shoved me in the direction of Smith, standing near the lamp. And the ladder.

"Can Wendy hold my hand? I... I don't want to die alone."

"You won't be, you stupid girl. Smith will be here, as will I." He laughed. "I suppose I'm already dead, so I don't count."

Wendy whimpered again. She looked terribly pale and I hoped she wouldn't faint on me.

"It's all right." I held out my hand to her. She clasped it tightly and I squeezed, trying to reassure her. Judging by her violent trembling, I had failed.

Smith clamped his hand over my nose and mouth. It was just like when he tried to kidnap me, back at the school, in London. His big paw cut off my air. His arms held me against the side of his body. I couldn't breathe. In a moment, I would faint. The master stood at the edge of the lamplight, grinning. He licked heavy lips and watched me die with those hard, cruel eyes of his. Eyes that I would never forget, in this life or the next.

CHAPTER 14

I felt for the pocket in my skirt, hidden by the folds of cotton. My bruised and battered hand shook until my fingers wrapped around deliciously cool metal. The comforting sensation brought a sense of otherworldly calm to my taut nerves. I could do this. I *needed* to do this; if not for me, then for Wendy.

I withdrew Mrs. Peeble's derringer pistol and shot Smith in the chest before he had time to register what I was doing. He fell to the floor, dead.

Wendy screamed, high and excruciatingly loud.

"Quiet!" I snapped. It may have sounded harsh, but I couldn't think with all that noise. She quieted instantly.

I didn't take my eyes off the master. He stood a few feet away, staring down at the dead man. A ripple of shock disturbed his pudgy features before he once more schooled himself.

"Did that make you feel better?" he drawled.

"Not particularly," I said. "I would rather he faced justice, but I could see no other way."

"Indeed." He stepped closer to me.

"Stay there."

"You won't shoot me." He took another step, watching me the entire time. Testing me, daring me to shoot. "This body doesn't deserve to die like Smith. It belongs to an innocent man. You're too moral for that. Too good. It's part of the reason why I adore you."

"Go up, Wendy," I told the whimpering girl. "Run. Get help." It would be too late by then. We all knew it. The master was right. I couldn't kill Butterworth. My only option was to somehow render him unconscious then escape and lock him in the basement.

To do that, I had to get close enough to hit him over the head with the pistol's handle, the only weapon at hand. Even then he could probably overpower me before I got in a single blow, or transfer into my body.

At least Wendy could get to safety. He wanted me, not her. She scampered up the ladder and opened the trapdoor. Daylight fell across the master's eyes. He paused and blinked.

I had a moment. No more. I spun round and began my ascent, even though I knew I wouldn't reach the top. He could close the gap between us faster than I could climb.

His laughter echoed around the basement. "Come here, stupid girl."

I'd reached the third rung when he grasped my ankle. He pulled. I kicked out and hung on to the ladder. He pulled down again, using his weight as an anchor. My fingers slipped as my sore hand screamed in agony. I couldn't hold on any longer. My heart pounded and tears of frustration and pain started anew. There was no means of escape. I was going to lose to the master. Again.

A dark object fell past my vision. It hit him with a sickening thud. He released my ankle and crumpled to ground without making a sound. Blood trickled from his temple and soaked into the floor. A brick lay nearby. Wendy must have dropped it through the trapdoor.

"Is he dead?" she called down.

"I... I don't know." A dead man couldn't die again. The spirit of the master was very much here, trapped in Butterworth's dead or unconscious body.

Unless he jumped to me.

I didn't know how close someone had to be for a spirit to transfer from one body to another, but I wasn't willing to find out. I scrambled up the ladder and out into the fresh air above ground. Wendy stood a little to the side, breathing heavily. Her eyes were swollen and red from crying, her hair tangled around her shoulders.

She wiped her nose and gave me a watery smile. "Thank you." She threw her thin arms around me and I hugged her, but just for a moment; there was still work to be done.

"Help me cover this trapdoor so he can't escape." I returned the pistol to my pocket and piled bricks onto the closed door. In a few short minutes, Wendy and I had built a tower that no man could dislodge from underneath.

"What do we do now?" she asked, dusting off her hands.

"You have to go for help."

She blinked. "Me? Alone?"

"You'll be all right. I have to stay here and ensure no one stumbles onto the... onto him." I refused to call him the master. He was *not* my master. He was nobody.

She stared out of the nearest glassless window. "Where are we?"

"I'm not sure. Somewhere near Harborough is my guess."

"Harborough? Is that close to London?" Her accent was what I called post-slum. She still possessed the harsh vowels of someone brought up in a rookery, but was attempting to cover it with a more refined accent she had yet to master. *He* would have taught her to speak like that, just like he'd taught me.

"Hertfordshire," I said. "Did you live in London with him?"

She wrapped her thin arms around herself. "Not him," she said, nodding at the trapdoor. "Another man. Another master. He had a big house in Mayfair. Beautiful, it was.

Then, two days ago, he ordered me to pack and we came here. We stayed in a house in the village."

"Mrs. Turner's house in Harborough?"

She nodded. "Then, this morning, that short, fat man visited. All friendly to us he was, and then suddenly he wasn't. He took me from the master and brought me here. Locked me down there." Her lower lip began to wobble. "I don't understand, miss. What's happened? Am I... free?"

I nodded.

She put her hands over her mouth to smother her sob. Her fingernails were filthy and broken. "But... the master? What if he comes here, too? I don't want to go back to him. I *hate* him."

The poor girl had been through enough. I wouldn't explain about the possession and frighten her further. "My friends went to the police to have him arrested. He should be locked away by now." Whoever he was, I hoped she would never see his face again. "You must go now, Wendy. Follow that road and any signs into Harborough or to Frakingham."

"Frakingham?"

"It's a large estate. My friends live there. They'll be looking for me, by now. They'll know what to do." Still she hesitated. "Wendy, you have to go. I would do it if you knew how to fire a gun." Or if I thought she had the willpower to stand up to anyone who might stumble upon us and demand the trapdoor be reopened.

She bit her lip. "I suppose."

"Just stay on the road. You'll be quite safe."

She finally left. I watched as she walked away from the house, casting a forlorn glance back at me. I gave her an encouraging smile. She had no shawl and wore a lovely pair of soft kid leather boots, not at all suitable for long country walks. The day was cool and the shadows grew long. I hoped she reached civilization before nightfall.

I settled myself into the window recess and pressed my temple against the rough brick. My mind wandered off, thinking of Samuel, Tommy and Sylvia. I hoped she was all right. It would have been convenient to have a vision now. If Samuel could see through my eyes, he might recognize the building site.

Something thudded against the trapdoor. I half-leaped, half-fell off the window embrasure. I stumbled and put my hand on the ground to stop myself falling completely. It was my bruised hand, the one Smith had stood on, and it hurt like the devil. I sucked air between my teeth and cradled it against my chest.

Thud, thud. "Bloody hell!" came Butterworth's muffled voice. "Let me out!"

I reached inside my pocket and withdrew the pistol. I returned to the window embrasure and rested the derringer on my lap, but kept it aimed at the trapdoor. I tried to shut out his shouts for help, but it wasn't easy. His shouts soon became panicked screams, then finally he quieted. He probably assumed Wendy and I had both left.

I waited. And waited. I scanned the road leading to the building site, but no one came. There were no sounds of wheels on the gravel, no police whistles. Just the rustle of the leaves of the forest trees and the chatter of birds settling in for the evening.

Once in a while the master called out, asking if anyone was there. He thumped on the trapdoor or grunted as he tried to shove the bricks off. Then he'd fall quiet again. Part of me wished he'd died, but that was pointless. He was already dead. The only way to remove him was to have Emily Beaufort or Cara send him back. It was a comfort to know they were on their way to Frakingham, and may have already arrived if they'd taken the train.

The sun dropped behind the forest and the air cooled. I shivered and wished I'd worn a warmer dress. Wendy should have found someone by now. Surely it couldn't take hours to walk to Harborough or Frakingham without meeting a soul. But what if she'd gotten lost?

An even more horrifying thought struck me. What if the master's spirit had transferred to her *before* she'd climbed out? What if I'd just allowed him to walk free and poor Mr. Butterworth was the one trapped down there?

I tried to think back to the events in the basement. When had she been close to the master? Had he still acted like himself right up until the moment the brick hit him? Or had the master, inside Wendy's body, aimed that brick at Butterworth on purpose to keep him quiet?

I was rifling through my jumbled thoughts when I heard the rumble of wheels on gravel. I spun round to see a familiar driver atop a familiar coach, Samuel beside him, half out of the seat.

He spotted me and almost jumped off while the coach still barreled along. He managed to wait until it had slowed down enough before he leapt down and ran to me.

I didn't get a chance to greet him or indeed say anything. He threw his arms around me and cradled me against his body. His warmth surrounded me, infused me. His rapidly beating heart thrummed through my body and echoed in my blood. He made me feel alive.

And yet so scared. He shouldn't be touching me. Not him. Not a man who could get what he wanted with mere words. Not someone with so much charm and far more power than a single man ought to have.

I pressed my uninjured hand to his chest and gently pushed. He broke away and part of me wanted to cry over the loss of his warmth and strength. But the rest of me needed the space between us. Craved it.

I pulled out of his arms completely. He didn't seem to notice my rejection. His gaze focused on the pile of bricks on top of the trapdoor. Muffled thumps sounded on the wood again.

"Is he in there?" asked Tommy. He'd joined us from the coach. Behind him stood Emily and Jacob Beaufort, the school's patrons. I smiled tentatively at Mrs. Beaufort, relieved beyond measure to see her sweet face, kind brown eyes, and her husband's strong, capable frame.

Then, suddenly, my face crumpled. My smile turned wobbly and tears spilled down my cheeks. I couldn't stop them and I began to shake uncontrollably. I could barely even wipe the tears away, my hand trembled so much.

Mrs. Beaufort folded me into her arms while Samuel looked on, his eyes bright, his mouth twisted as he struggled to hold in his emotions. I buried my face in Mrs. Beaufort's shoulder so that I didn't have to look at him.

I heard the men pulling off the bricks and throwing them aside. The master must have heard it, too. His thuds became more frantic, his shouts filled with hope. Nobody answered him when he asked who was there.

When all the bricks were gone and only Samuel and Tommy stood on the trapdoor to keep it shut, Mr. Beaufort turned to his wife.

"Ready?" he asked.

She nodded and let me go to join her husband. "Let him out," she said.

Tommy stepped off. Samuel did not. He lowered his head and closed his fists at his sides. He was hatless and his hair fell across his forehead, covering his eyes.

My heart tugged. I wanted to go to him, but I hung back, uncertain. Mr. Beaufort rested his hand on Samuel's shoulder. Samuel huffed out a breath and moved off the trapdoor.

It sprang back and Butterworth's head popped out. He blinked in the dusky light and stared up at the men surrounding him. "Who are you?" he asked as he climbed out. It was a trick. He knew who Samuel was.

Mrs. Beaufort, standing a little behind her husband, began to chant the words that would banish the spirit. Mr. Beaufort's body was rigid, ready to stop Butterworth getting too close to her if necessary.

Butterworth's face fell. His cold, dead eyes fixed on me. "Bitch," he snarled. He'd barely even gotten the word out when Samuel grasped his jacket lapels and shook him violently.

"Gladstone!" Mr. Beaufort shouted. "Are you mad? Let him go!"

Samuel pulled back his fist to take a swing at Butterworth.

Tommy grabbed it. "He'll possess you!" he shouted. "Move away!"

Samuel shook him off and landed a punch on Butterworth's nose. Butterworth swayed backwards as blood spurted down his face and onto his collar. He swiped at it with the back of his hand, smearing blood over his cuff.

He laughed. "You're the fellow who's been enjoying *my* Charity. You should thank me for training her good and proper."

Samuel bared his teeth. A low growl rumbled in the base of his chest, primal and fierce. He pulled back his fist to throw another punch, but Butterworth suddenly crumpled. He sat heavily on the floor and rolled onto his side, groaning into his hands.

It was over. The master's spirit was gone.

So why was Mrs. Beaufort still chanting?

Samuel approached me and held out his hand. "Come with me, my love." It was Samuel's voice yet not. It didn't have the same cadence, the same lyrical, rich tones. And his eyes weren't Samuel's. They were harder, colder, deader.

The master was now inside him.

I stumbled backward, away from him. Away from Samuel. Beyond him, Tommy seemed unaware of what had happened. He looked down at Butterworth, still on the floor. Only the Beauforts seemed to know that the spirit had transferred. Mrs. Beaufort continued to concentrate, but her husband appeared torn between staying near his wife and helping me.

I stopped and squared up to my tormentor. My voice shook, but I spoke as firmly as possible. "Who are you? What's your name?"

He merely grinned. "My name isn't important, but I was once a powerful man, Charity. You remember that, don't you? The power of my belt on your back. You loved it. You *wanted* it."

I held myself tight, keeping my fears inside. Fear would cripple me and I needed to know one more thing. "Who is the medium who helped you?"

Samuel's beautiful mouth twisted into a slick sneer. "We had an agreement. I won't tell if she won't."

Mrs. Beaufort stopped. Her last words drifted away on the breeze blowing through the building. Samuel staggered a little. His shoulders drooped, his head hung low.

"It's done," she said. "He's gone."

My weak legs couldn't hold me anymore. I plopped down on the floor and buried my face in my skirts. My tears flowed freely, but I made no sound. It's how I'd cried when living with *him*.

Mrs. Beaufort's arm circled my shoulders. "It's over, now. You can return home."

Home. The school. The children. My heart lifted a little, but it still felt so heavy. Would that heaviness ever completely go away?

She helped me to stand. Tommy assisted a dazed Butterworth to his feet. The mayor blinked at the faces around him and asked question after question. Mr. Beaufort told him he'd suffered an illness that had caused him to lose his memory.

"And my nose to bleed?" He touched his nose and winced in pain. "My head aches like the devil."

"You fell."

He looked around, taking in his surroundings. "What are we doing at my future house?"

"Inspecting it," Tommy said, steering Butterworth out of the building. "Come with me, sir. We'll take you home."

They walked out, followed by the Beauforts, his arm around her waist as if he didn't want to let her go. He kissed her forehead and she smiled up at him.

They seemed to think that I would want Samuel to walk me out. He hadn't moved since the spirit had left him. He still stood there with his head hanging low, but he watched me from behind the strands of his hair.

"Are you all right?" I asked.

"I should be asking you that."

I tucked my injured hand behind my back before I realized what I was doing. I didn't want his tenderness and concern. Didn't want him to touch me.

Yet, at the same time, I did.

I swallowed and turned away to follow the others out to the coach.

"Charity." I stopped and glanced back at him over my shoulder. His chest rose with his breathing. "You've remembered, haven't you? The block has worn off?"

I nodded.

"Where's the brute? Smith?"

So he did know his name. "Down there. He's dead." I rushed out of the building, not wanting to have a conversation with him alone. But I didn't turn away fast enough, and saw the sadness touch his eyes and the shadows return.

I hurried to the coach. Samuel took a few more minutes to join us. I suspected he'd gone down to the basement to check Smith. He emerged from the building and sat outside with the driver and Tommy. There was only room for the Beauforts, Mr. Butterworth and me in the cabin. The last time I'd been in a coach with the mayor, I'd been terrified. Now I saw him for the pathetic man he was without the master possessing him.

The building site was indeed not far from Harborough. We must have driven around the village on our way to it, but I'd not seen, cowering as I was on the floor. We deposited Butterworth at his home, giving his wife instructions to call the doctor. With him gone, Samuel could once more sit inside and we were able to talk freely.

"Jacob and I arrived a short while ago, by train," Mrs. Beaufort told me. "We were met at the station by Samuel and Tommy—they were frantic. Apparently they'd returned from investigating a house in the village to find you kidnapped."

"Mrs. Turner's," Samuel said. He seemed somewhat calmer than before, more in control of his emotions. He did not look directly at me, however. "We found a very dazed gentleman there. He claimed to have been missing a few *years* of his memory."

"Years?" I whispered. "The poor man."

"It was the master in his guise who lured that girl in," Samuel said.

"Wendy. You found her? Is she all right?"

He nodded. "She wandered into the village around the time we met the Beauforts at the station. She told us how to find you and I sent her on to Frakingham. Sylvia will take care of her."

I was relieved beyond measure to know she was safe and well. "She saved me, saved us both. She dropped a brick on Butterworth's head."

Mrs. Beaufort's brows rose. "That explains the egg on his temple and the blood."

"What of the other man?" her husband asked.

"He's dead," Samuel said. "Shot."

"Shot!" Mrs. Beaufort's big brown eyes turned to me. "You had a gun?"

I retrieved the derringer from my pocket. "Mrs. Peeble gave it to me before I left London, with strict instructions to have it on me at all times. I didn't heed her advice that night Smith tried to kidnap me from my room at Frakingham. I have ever since."

"Mrs. Peeble is rather an indomitable woman," Mrs. Beaufort said on a sigh. "I suppose I shouldn't chastise her for having a weapon in the school, since it worked out for the best, but it is dangerous near the children."

"She doesn't keep it loaded and it's in her room the entire time."

"Thank goodness for that."

***

Sylvia, Myer, Langley and Bollard met us in the entrance hall when we arrived at the house. "Thank God," Sylvia murmured, hugging me. "You're in one piece. I was so worried. We all were. Poor Samuel was beside himself when he returned to find you gone." She touched a hand to the back of her head and winced.

"Are you all right?" I asked.

"I have a headache that feels like it's trying to crack my skull open. But it will pass."

"Where's Wendy?"

"Having a bath, then she's going to bed. She's exhausted, poor thing."

To my surprise, Langley wheeled himself over and clasped my hand in his. "I am glad to see you looking well, Charity. You gave us quite a scare."

Bollard, standing behind him, gave me a smile that crinkled his eyes and softened his mouth. Even Myer's equine features drew together in concern. Tommy headed to the service area while we made our way into the drawing room.

"I met Gladstone on the road as he and the footman headed to the Turner woman's house," Myer said once we were all seated. "I was more than happy to offer assistance and we traveled there together. We found the fellow disoriented and quite harmless. We quickly realized the spirit had transferred to Butterworth. I must tell you, Miss Evans, it was quite the dramatic turn of events. We were all concerned for your welfare. Gladstone returned to Frakingham while I remained to see to the gentleman's immediate comfort, then I came here some time later and waited. Has the spirit been sent back?" he asked Mrs. Beaufort.

She nodded.

"Did you recognize him?"

It was a question I was curious to know the answer to myself. I knew the master only by that name, but he could very well have been someone from their circle. He certainly lived in comfort.

"No," Mrs. Beaufort said. "Whoever he was, he has returned to the Waiting Area, where the Administrators will keep a better eye on him until he crosses. He shouldn't cause any more harm."

"Shouldn't?" Samuel echoed. "That doesn't sound definitive."

"Nothing is definitive when it comes to the supernatural," Myer said. "You ought to know that, Gladstone. Your memory block, for one thing. Has it completely worn off now, Miss Evans?"

"Yes." I stared down at my folded hands. The injured one still throbbed a little.

Tommy entered and passed around cups of warm chocolate. He did not immediately let go of Sylvia's, but allowed their fingers to touch longer than appropriate. I didn't have the energy to scowl my disapproval at him. He wasn't looking at me anyway, only at her.

"There is one odd thing," Myer said. When Myer said something was odd, it must definitely be strange. We all looked to him.

"What is it?" Mr. Beaufort asked, somewhat impatiently. I got the impression he and his wife didn't particularly like the man.

"I recognized him," Myer said.

"Who?" Samuel asked.

"The man at Mrs. Turner's house. It took me a while to place him, and indeed I had to ask him his name to fully solve the puzzle. He's Charles Clement, the general manager of Clement and Co."

"The bank?" Mr. Beaufort sat forward. "I know him. He belongs to my club, but he's rarely been there of late. Indeed, he's not been there for two or three years."

"Since the possession," I muttered. I shivered and Sylvia pressed her hand over mine, reassuring.

"It was rumored that he'd gone a little mad," Mr. Beaufort went on. "He'd been making some poor business decisions of late too, erratic ones, when before he'd been careful and clever."

"The master was not a banker, then," Mrs. Beaufort said. "Nor did he have any interest in the company, it would seem."

"Or any interest in keeping Mr. Clement's reputation in good standing."

"Mr. Clement is going to have quite a shock when he re-enters his old life," Sylvia said. "His work will have altered dramatically, for one thing."

"Clement and Co. is a rival bank to your own, Myer, is it not?" Samuel asked.

Myer nodded. "I'd heard the same rumors as Mr. Beaufort. The general manager was making poor decisions, sending the bank into decline, that sort of thing. He'll have an enormous task ahead of him to rectify the situation and redeem himself."

"Indeed," Mrs. Beaufort echoed.

"That's if he can recover from what has happened to him at all," Myer said quietly. "There are some things that, no matter how hard we try, we will never be free from."

He wasn't looking at me, but I knew with deep certainty that he was talking about my situation. I wanted to disagree with him. I wanted to tell him that people could recover from anything if they desired it enough and worked toward that end.

But I was proof that even a strong spirit could collapse under the weight of horrific memories and never fully recover. I had changed, unutterably, at the master's hands. No matter how hard I tried, I could never go back to being that carefree girl I'd been before he trapped me.

Not even erasing those memories had freed me entirely. Nor had his death. I would never be capable of trusting a man, never be able to offer love or fully accept it in return. Never be free of the nightmares that haunted me.

CHAPTER 15

The morning dawned clear, despite overnight rain. Drops hung like crystals from the leaves of the weeping willows down by the lake. It was a morning that promised a beautiful spring day ahead. A morning for fresh starts and bright futures. The morning on which I would leave Frakingham.

I walked from the lake to the ruins, contemplating my future. I wanted to wander around them before Myer arrived to continue his studies. It was peaceful in the still air, the sweet smell of blossoms and damp earth making me regret that I would be departing the countryside and once more returning to the smoke-choked city. Sylvia and Tommy had both begged me to stay longer, but I didn't like to impose, and I wanted to see the children again.

Samuel had said nothing after I announced I would catch the train back to London with the Beauforts and Wendy, a mere two days after Mrs. Beaufort had sent the master away. He had seemed on edge ever since, and had hardly spoken to me. Indeed, he rarely even looked at me. I was beginning to think he was avoiding my presence altogether, until he followed me down to the ruins.

I knew it was he, even at a distance, from the fairness of his head and the bright white of his shirt. He'd taken to not wearing a waistcoat or jacket around the house, preferring to don only his shirt, despite Sylvia's pleas that he dress appropriately around the guests. I thought the disregard for convention very unlike him. It had me worried, although not worried enough to question him over it. In truth, I was avoiding him, too.

But there would be no avoiding him now. His step had purpose. He wanted to speak to me. I braced myself, and prepared my own little speech. There were things that needed to be said before I could return home.

"Good morning," I said. "It's a beautiful morning for a walk."

He squinted into the sky and blinked rapidly as if the sun hurt his eyes. "When do you leave?"

"In an hour."

He inclined his head in a nod. I waited for him to speak again, but he said nothing more. He folded his arms over his chest then unfolded them and let them hang loose at his sides again. He flicked his fingernail, over and over, with his thumb. It was a maddening habit and after a while I could focus on nothing else.

I caught his hand to still it. The connection arrowed his intense gaze onto me. I felt like I could see through to his soul and he into mine. I saw his weariness, his desire, his fears.

They were my fears, reflected back at me.

I withdrew my hand. He closed his fist like a sunflower going to sleep at night. "I don't want you to be afraid of me," he whispered, as if he were reluctant to say it aloud.

I was about to tell him I wasn't, but we both knew it wasn't true. There was no point lying to Samuel. He knew me too well. Of course I was afraid of him. He had almost hypnotized me without even trying.

"I'll never hurt you, Charity."

I should tell him that I knew that. I should tell him a great many things. I'd prepared a speech... "Samuel, I'm sorry I asked you to block my memories. If I'd known—"

"Don't. Don't apologize. It's not your fault."

"But I've given you a burden you shouldn't have to carry. It was selfish of me to ask such a thing of you. Cowardly."

He put up his hands, warding off my words. "It's not your memories that shock or burden me, it's your memories and mine together."

He'd said a similar thing before, but he'd been reluctant to elaborate. "What do you mean?"

He shook his head, dismissing my question. He was still reluctant then.

"Tell me, Samuel. It's only fair that I should carry your burden since you are helping to carry mine."

The corner of his mouth kicked up in a tired smile. "I'm not sure I've been any help at all."

"You have. You brought me here and sheltered me. You protected me from… from him."

He shook his head. "You did that. You were very brave, Charity. But I wish you'd informed me of your plan."

It didn't feel like bravery, just necessity. "I knew you wouldn't allow me to go ahead with it. Besides, I thought it the best way to save Wendy and capture the master. Even so, he did catch me unawares in the guise of Butterworth. Informing you of my plan wouldn't have made any difference. He tricked us both."

"I've known fear before, but never fear on that scale. When I realized what had happened…" He swallowed heavily and twisted his head to the side as if he were turning away from a gruesome sight.

I wanted to reach for him, comfort him, but hung back. Touching him would open up a flood of emotions, for both him and me, and I couldn't cope with that sort of intimacy between us.

There was nothing more to say and it was time for me to prepare to leave Frakingham. "Goodbye, Samuel. Thank you, for everything."

I went to walk off, but he stepped in front of me. His eyes were two dark swirling orbs, his breathing labored. He reached out to take my hand, but seemed to collect himself at the last moment and dashed his fingers through his hair instead. "Don't," he choked out. "Don't say goodbye. This isn't goodbye."

"Please don't make this harder than it already is." My whispered plea caught me by surprise. I thought I wanted to return to London—and I did, in part. But there was a piece of me that wanted to remain within the safe walls of Frakingham, with people I'd grown to like, if not fully trust.

But that was hiding away, and I'd had enough of hiding and running. Besides, the children needed me and I needed them.

"You must understand that I'll do everything I can to protect you," he said.

"Thank you," I said, my throat tight. "But you've done enough. Don't worry about me. I'll be all right. He's gone now."

"What if he's not?" His shouted words forced me backwards. "Well? What if his spirit comes back?"

"He's gone," I whispered.

"Mrs. Beaufort isn't sure."

Tears sprang to my eyes. What if he was right? What if the master came back?

"Bollocks," he muttered. "This isn't coming out right." He sucked in a deep breath. It seemed to calm him a little, although the wildness didn't completely vanish from his eyes. "Even if *he* doesn't return, there are other dangers for a woman alone. I don't want them to touch you, Charity," he said softly. "I want to protect you, not only from physical harm, but all ills."

"I'll be fine."

"A woman alone is too easy a target," he went on as if I hadn't spoken. He was talking rapidly now, like a madman intent on getting the words out. It troubled me to see him so agitated. He was nothing like the Samuel Gladstone I knew from our first meetings. The charm had vanished, replaced by something far more fierce and intense, but no less frightening.

He suddenly caught my hand and dropped to one knee before I'd even registered what he was doing.

"Marry me, Charity," he said. "Marry me and let me protect you."

LOOK OUT FOR

Seared With Scars

The second book in the second FREAK HOUSE
TRILOGY.

To be notified when C.J. has a new release, sign up to her
newsletter. Send an email to cjarcher.writes@gmail.com

ABOUT THE AUTHOR

C.J. Archer has loved history and books for as long as she can remember. She worked as a librarian and technical writer until she was able to channel her twin loves by writing historical fiction. She has won and placed in numerous romance writing contests, including taking home RWAustralia's Emerald Award in 2008 for the manuscript that would become her novel *Honor Bound*. Under the name Carolyn Scott, she has published contemporary romantic mysteries, including *Finders Keepers Losers Die*, and *The Diamond Affair*. After spending her childhood surrounded by the dramatic beauty of outback Queensland, she lives today in suburban Melbourne, Australia, with her husband and their two children.

She loves to hear from readers. You can contact her in one of these ways:
Website: www.cjarcher.com
Email: cjarcher.writes@gmail.com
Facebook: www.facebook.com/CJArcherAuthorPage

13562452R00126

Printed in Great Britain
by Amazon.co.uk, Ltd.,
Marston Gate.